Moored in a coastal fishing town so far north that the highways only run south, the unnamed narrator of *The Seas* is a misfit. She's often the subject of cruel local gossip. Her father, a sailor, walked into the ocean eleven years earlier and never returned, leaving his wife and daughter to keep a forlorn vigil. Surrounded by water and beckoned by the sea, she clings to what her father once told her: that she is a mermaid.

True to myth, she finds herself in hard love with a land-bound man, an Iraq War veteran thirteen years her senior. The mesmerizing, fevered coming-of-age tale that follows will land her in jail. Her otherworldly escape will become the stuff of legend.

With the inventive brilliance and psychological insight that have earned her international acclaim, Samantha Hunt pulls readers into an undertow of impossible love and intoxication, blurring the lines between reality and fairy tale, hope and delusion, sanity and madness.

PRAISE FOR *The Seas*

"An aqueous affair, flooded with water themes. It's the kind of novel in which King Neptune and several mermaids put in appearances, and which leaves no metaphor unrealized—the woman falls on some scattered movable type and is bruised by words. In other hands, this might all feel distinctly soggy, but Hunt's writing is free of affectation and carries surprising conviction."

—THE NEW YORKER

"Urgently real and magically unreal... A breathy, wonderful holler of a novel, deeply lodged in the ocean's merciless blue ... [Hunt] sinks an anchor into the soul of its lost young protagonist."

—THE VILLAGE VOICE

"To describe Samantha Hunt's entrancing first novel, *The Seas*, is to try to interpret a watery dream that pushes the boundaries between fiction and fantasy. . . . Hunt's nimbleness makes the idea of leaning toward mermaid fantasies enticing."

—*SAN FRANCISCO CHRONICLE*

"Samantha Hunt! Yes. She's completely original, one of the most distinctive and unforgettable voices I've read in years. This book will linger, like something wet and smelly from the sea, in your head for a good long time. Unlike something wet and smelly, you will like the lingering of this thing."

—DAVE EGGERS

THE SEAS

Published by Tin House Books, Portland, Oregon, and
Brooklyn, New York

Distributed by W. W. Norton & Company

Library of Congress Cataloging-in-Publication Data

Names: Hunt, Samantha, author.
Title: The seas : a novel / by Samantha Hunt.
Description: Cage Tin House edition. | Portland, OR : Tin
House Books, 2018.
Identifiers: LCCN 2018003452 | ISBN 9781941040959
Subjects: | GSAFD: Love stories. | Sea stories.
Classification: LCC PS3608.U585 S43 2018 | DDC 813/.6--
dc23
LC record available at https://lccn.loc.gov/2018003452

Printed in the USA
Interior design by Diane Chonette
www.tinhouse.com

THE SEAS

SAMANTHA HUNT

Tin House Books
Portland, Oregon & Brooklyn, New York

For Walter and Diane

TABLE OF CONTENTS

INTRODUCTION

I read *The Seas* when it first came out and was scalded by its beauty. It took me back to how I felt as a kid, when you're newly falling in love with literature, newly shocked by its capacity to cast a spell—you know the feeling, when you turn the last page of a novel that you've burrowed into and has burrowed into you, and suddenly find that the book has become more than a book, it's become a talisman, something precious. A little scary, a little holy.

The Seas felt like that to me. Radiant with magic, some of it dangerous. Some of it hurt. Probably I feared it a bit—not only how perfect it was, as a piece of writing, but also how much it made me feel. About the gigantic, all-consuming blue wave that begins and ends and haunts *The Seas*, our nineteen-year-old narrator writes: "It is truly a gorgeous color. This blue is chaotic and changing. I recognize it immediately." I recognized, recognize, it too. It's the wave that holds the narrator's grief for her lost father, her wobbly faith in language and etymology, her enthrallment with the oceanic, her fixation on the color blue, her complex relationship to her mother, her bobbing amidst a sea of alcoholics, her own fierce sexual desire, her loneliness, her conviction of her mermaid nature, her love for a mortal in deep pain whose suffering mirrors, alleviates, and exacerbates her own. It's the wave that reveals the painful, exhilarating scope of her small and swelling life. O that wave.

And so I put *The Seas* up on a high shelf, not because I didn't love it, but because its power felt so acute I needed to dim it a little, save it for another day.

Its re-release thankfully provided that occasion.

And so I took it down, read it again in one sitting, then read it again the next day, and then one more the next, each time finding it as mesmerizing, moving, and crystalline as I did years ago.

Like so much of her work since, Hunt's storytelling here performs a mysterious balancing act between the so-called real and the so-called fantastical, making words like "magical realism," "surrealism," "allegory," or "fairytale" swirl around her work. I read *The Seas* a little differently, however. I read it as a portrait of human psychology that imagines human emotion as an elemental force on par with air, water, wind, and fire. Seen this way, whatever is "not real" in *The Seas* could also be read as a deep, perhaps the deepest, sort of realism—a vision akin to, say, the penetrating insight of shamanistic trance.

On the other hand, there also exists the real possibility throughout that the narrator of *The Seas* is not just unreliable but quite possibly insane, drifting further and further toward a destructive psychosis. Such uncertainty pulses in lines such as: "He is gone and the water rushes up behind me like a couple of police officers with their blue lights flashing, with their steel-blue guns drawn." It will take 150 more pages for the reader to fathom the nature of that simile, and even then, there will be room to wonder.

As its nesting-doll epigraph suggests (*It was a dark and stormy night, / and the ship was on the sea. / The captain said, "Sailor, tell us a story," / and the sailor began, / "It was a dark and stormy night, / and the ship was at sea . . ."*), *The Seas* has what we once might have called "postmodern" structure, in terms of its attention to stories within stories, and its slow, perhaps even deconstructive inquiry into the granular nature of language itself, even down to the atomistic nature of individual letters. But as its epigraph also suggests, there's a certain ancient, Scheherazade-like framing at work here as well. Despite the occasional entrance of historical markers (the carnies with tattooed teardrops, the details of the Iraq War, the sociologists visiting the oceanside town to study its high rates of alcoholism), the story of *The Seas* is timeless, archetypal. A tale of love and war.

A tale of love and war that is narrated, importantly, by a woman. *The Seas* never fails to bring to my mind the work of visionary poet Alice Notley, who has "channeled" her dead father, who died of alcoholism, and her dead brother, a Vietnam vet traumatized by the war, as a means of composing long poems. I think of how, after writing these works, Notley says she grew impatient with the woman's role as "essentially passive: sufferer, survivor." What do women *do*, Notley wondered, besides serve as witness? Eventually Notley came up with the following answer: "Insomuch as woman dream, they participate in stories every night of their lives. Profound stories which may involve sex, death, violence, journeys, quests, all the stuff of epic & much of narrative." Against the idea that dreams have relevance only on the margins of psychic or historical life, Notley argues that "life is a dream; that we construct reality in a dreamlike way; that we agree to be in the same dream; and that the only way to change reality is to recognize its dreamlike qualities and act as if it is malleable."

Such questions, along with Notley's answers, seem to me at the heart of *The Seas*, in which Hunt showcases her own uncanny ability to "recognize [reality's] dreamlike qualities and act as if it is malleable." While our narrator may be subsumed by Jude's trauma, her desire for him is sharply wrought, and all her own: "Some nights I want Jude so badly that I imagine I am giving birth to him. I pretend to sweat. I toss and wring my insides out. Mostly I think this because that's how badly I want Jude's head between my legs." "Jude thinks he is too old for me. I think I could cut a strip of flesh from his upper arm and eat it." And (spoiler alert) just as *The Seas* seems to merge her and Jude's tragic fates, echoing the countless romantic narratives in which true love means (literally, in this case) drowning in one another's sorrows, our narrator pulls out ahead, starts swimming toward a different future. (I think she does, anyway—there's room to wonder here as well.) In a way that feels entirely earned and also surprising, *The Seas* edges away from the consuming whirlpools of drunk, dead father and drunk, tortured ex-soldier, and toward a fresh reckoning between a living mother and her living daughter, not to mention between a young woman and herself.

Since *The Seas*, Hunt has written two ambitious novels and a collection of short stories, all of which demonstrate her ever-deepening access to the strange, the inventive, the magic, and the dark—indeed, the "dark dark," as in the title of her most recent collection. I love and admire all of this work, but *The Seas* will always occupy a special place for me, standing, as it does, on a precipice overlooking deep reserves of desire, liminality, mystery, and pain. Do you know that song by Björk, "Anchor Song"? Go look it up, and listen to it alongside *The Seas*. "Anchor Song" is a simple, seaside anthem—another plainspoken, adamant claim, made by a woman speaking with formidable grace and power.

And yet. For all its insistence on remaining seaside—for all the ways in which *The Seas* offers an incisive, compassionate portrait of how and why we don't get out of our fucked-up towns, our fucked-up loves, our fucked-up families, our fucked-up habits, our fucked-up homes, and our fucked-up wars—perhaps what's most remarkable about it is how in the end it illuminates—seemingly against all odds—a means of getting out.

MAGGIE NELSON

Los Angeles, 2017

THE SEAS

It was a dark and stormy night,
and the ship was on the sea.
The captain said, "Sailor, tell us a story,"
and the sailor began.
"It was a dark and stormy night,
and the ship was on the sea . . ."

THE MAP: A PROLOGUE

The highway only goes south from here. That's how far north we live. There aren't many roads out of town, which explains why so few people ever leave. Things that are unfamiliar are a long way off and there is no direct route to these things. Rather it's a street to a street to a road across a causeway to a road across a bridge to a road to another road before you reach the highway.

If you were to try to leave, people who have known you since the day you were born would recognize your car and see you leaving. They would wonder where you were going and they would wave with two fingers off the steering wheel, a wave that might seem like a stop sign or a warning to someone trying to forget this very small town. It would be much easier to stay.

The town is built on a steep and rocky coast so that the weathered houses are stacked like shingles, or like the rows of razor wire in a prison, one on top of the other up the hill. Small paths and narrow roads wind their ways between the houses so that there's no privacy in this town. If you were to stumble home drunk one night, by morning, the entire town would know. Not that they would care. People here are accustomed to drunks. We have the highest rate of alcoholism in the country, and this fact is repeated so often I thought we should put it on the Chamber of Commerce sign at the town line that welcomes tourists. *More alcoholics per capita! Enjoy your visit!*

Most of the waterfront is cluttered with moorings, piers that smell of motor oil, and outbuildings for the fishermen, though there is a short stretch of sandy beach and a boardwalk where every summer a few fool tourists fail to enjoy themselves and spend their vacations wondering why anyone would live here. If they asked me I'd tell them, "We live here because we hate the rest of you." Though that isn't always true, it is sometimes.

Then there is the ocean, mean and beautiful.

"We're getting out of here," I say. "Let's go." I find Jude's keys on his kitchen table. He is still in the living room, just lying there. Underneath the keys on the table there is a pen and a letter written from Jude to me. His handwriting is like his hair, long and dark tangles. The letter is tucked into an envelope where Jude has written on the outside:

THE REST OF THE STORY

I stuff the envelope into my jacket pocket, being careful not to fold or crush it. "I'll drive," I say, leaving the door open for Jude. I pull myself up into the driver's seat and rasp the bench forward. "Jude," I call. I start the truck. It will be hundreds of miles before I have to decide where we are actually going. For now we are just going south.

I can't see anything besides rain. The back window is blurred by droplets and fogging up with our breath. "Would you turn on the defrost?" I ask him, but he doesn't move. He just stares out the window. I do it myself and a blast of cool air from outside floods the truck. The air smells like a terrific storm that came all the way from secret strata high up in the atmosphere, a place so far away it smells unlike the tarred scent of sea decay we have here.

I feel buoyant. I feel light and ready. I feel like we are getting out of here and mostly I feel Jude inside me and it feels like love.

Jude is being very quiet but that is not unusual. Jude has been quiet over the past year and a half, ever since he returned home from the war. He is closing his eyes so as not to see the land we know disappearing. From here, if there were no rain, we would see how our poor town sits in a pit of sadness, like a black hole or a wallowing cavity or an old woman. We would see how the town stares out at the ocean it loves, never considering its other options. The town must be drunk to love the ocean because the ocean thinks the town is small and weak. The ocean always beats the town throughout the hardest winter months, pulling down houses and ripping up boats.

In the rearview there's just rain and so we can't see anything. I feel free. I give the truck a little gas, trying to increase the distance between us and back there. "Jude," I say, "we're getting out of here."

I look again in the rearview mirror and quite suddenly there is a beautiful blue, as though the storm finally broke. It is truly a gorgeous color. This blue is chaotic and changing. I recognize it immediately. "Jude," I say. "Look," and I point into the rearview mirror. "It's the ocean sneaking up behind us." I watch as the blue rises up like a tidal wave so quickly that I am certain it will catch up with us soon. "It doesn't want us to leave." I check the mirror. "I don't think we can outrun the ocean but I'll try for your sake." I accelerate. I look again in the rearview. The color blue fills the entire mirror and, watching it, I think that is how a small northern town in America works. It enlists one beautiful thing like the ocean or the mountains or the snow to keep people stuck and stagnant and staring out to sea forever.

I watch the blue in the mirror. It is so gorgeous, it is hard to look away. "Jude," I say, "all right. Fuck the dry land. I am a mermaid." I turn to look at him, to see what he will think of that, but Jude is not sitting beside me. "Jude?" I stare at the empty vinyl seat where he should be. He is not there. He is gone. I reach my hand over to touch the empty seat and even glance down underneath the seat looking for him. I look away from the road for too long. He is gone and the water rushes up behind me like a couple of police officers with their blue lights flashing, with their steel-blue guns drawn.

UNABRIDGED

"I'm not from here, am I?" I ask my mother while she tightens the strap of her bathrobe. I don't want to be from here because most of the people in this town think of me as a mold or a dangerous fungus that might infect their basements. I am the town's bad seed. I am their rotten heart.

My mother opens her robe a crack so I can see the loose elastic of her pink underwear and her belly button. It is popped and spread as a manhole. "Look at that," she says and points to her stretched stomach as evidence. "That's where you're from, nineteen years ago," she says.

"Dad said I came from the water."

"That certainly would be unusual."

My mother is regularly torn between being herself and being my mother. Her internal argument is sometimes visible from the outside, as if she had two heads sprouting from her one neck. The heads bicker like sisters. One says, "Be sensible for your daughter's sake. Three meals a day. Brush teeth at night. Organize. Comet. Pledge. Joy." While the other head says nothing. The other head is reading a book about whether life exists outside our solar system.

She glances across the kitchen to my grandfather for his reaction. He doesn't make one. I have grown to count on his abiding distraction. Having my grandfather in the house is like having a secret tunnel open to the distant past, where he lives.

My grandfather stirs the sugar in the sugar bowl, staring at the kitchen door where the neighbor's cat plucks the screen with her claw. The man who owns the cat is a strange man. The cat often comes over to our house for a bowl of water as the man only serves the cat orange juice or ginger ale or milk. The man is afraid of water. He doesn't drink it and washes minimally. The man was once a sailor who survived a very bad storm. He says he saw the water do things that night that he doesn't bother to repeat anymore because no one would believe him. But it must have been bad because he hasn't gone out on the sea for years and still he can start to tremble with fear if my mother turns on her garden hose to water the impatiens.

The cat plucks the screen. "Dad said I'm a mermaid," I tell them.

"But mermaids don't have legs or a voice or a soul unless they marry a mortal," my mother says. My mother listens to my voice. My mother looks at my legs. "You don't even have a husband."

"Ma. Urruggg." I'm annoyed because she's pointing out many of the very same things I've already heard. They rub a raw spot.

"I see." She rocks her back against the kitchen counter.

"But I don't see so well. And I think my trouble seeing might be a characteristic of the depth of the sea where I am from. It is a region so dark blue the creatures from that depth have no pigment and neither do their eyes. Like me." I look away from them, out the door. "There are some creatures down there who don't even have eyes at all."

My grandfather stops stirring the sugar. "I've got a word for that place." He wheels his office chair over to the windowsill where he keeps one of many dictionaries. He throws the book open on the table. It makes a good thud. He leafs through the pages very quickly. "I can almost remember the word. It starts with *had-* or *ha-*. I read it in the *Scientific American* a few years ago and I looked it up at the time." He tears through the dictionary searching for the word that means

  –n. a region of deep sea so dark that the creatures
  who dwell there have little or no pigment

"It was here," he says. "Someone took it," he says, and looks at my mother and me with suspicion, mostly me.

I try not to meet his gaze but he's a tough old man, my father's father, and he can stare at me for a long time. Eventually I have to look away. I walk over to the screen door and let the kitty cat inside.

I was thirsty. It was just floating there. And anyway, that word is mine.

THE SCIENTIFIC AMERICAN

The first day I met Jude, I was wading in the ocean. This was long before he joined the Army. Maybe I was twelve or thirteen at the time. When I looked up, Jude was swimming near the shore. He looked like a horse. A seahorse. There he is, I thought and meant my father, because I had been waiting for him to come back. And then I had a thought. I am very interested in science and I had heard about two different theoretical experiments that seem to demonstrate similar principles. The first was that if a bunch of monkeys were locked in a room with a typewriter, eventually they would produce the entire works of William Shakespeare. This sounded like an excellent experiment to me. It made me want to be a scientist. The second experiment I had heard of was that, in quantum physics, the possibility exists that one day the molecules of a body could arrange themselves just so that a person would be able to pass through a wall that appears solid to the eye. That is how much room we have between our molecules. I thought of that then I thought, "This is the place where all of my father's molecules went." Then Jude was coming out of the water and I thought, in quantum physics there must be a possibility that all the molecules of my father would find each other again and would walk out of the water looking at least a little bit like him.

But Jude didn't walk out of the water. He stayed there for a long time and he must have been freezing because the ocean this far north is rarely suited for swimming though some children do. But this man didn't look like a child. Tall and dark, he looked like my father. There, at that moment, I started loving Jude.

"Hello," I yelled to him. He turned towards me, looked a long time, shook his head, and waved. "What are you doing?"

"Looking for something."

Me too. "Me too," I said, but the waves were very loud between us.

Finally Jude walked towards me. His lips were turning blue like a drowned man's. This far north horrible things happen all the time to young girls but I wasn't afraid of him. He seemed sad, so, kinder in his sadness.

"You look like you've been in the water forever," I said.

He stood where the waves began to break, where what was blue became white, a sheet of paper roiling with all that had been written there. Jude kept walking towards me. "My name is Jude." So I saw he was not my father, but barely.

"How come I don't know you?" I asked. The town is small enough. Everybody knows everybody else.

We watched the water between us. "You do now." The water rushed back out to sea and the ocean filled up with words, like Jude was bleeding all the things he couldn't tell anyone because it might kill him. The rest of the story.

The strip of stores for tourists and the small amusement park beside the ocean stretch only as far as the sandy beach does. On either end of the strip the coast becomes rocky again. The strip is what keeps the town in business, that and an iron works for shipbuilding that once got a government contract back in the 1970s and so continues to operate, holding out hope that one day something like that might happen again.

I sometimes sit underneath our small boardwalk. It's out of the weather, away from anyone who might recognize me, close to the ocean. There I feel as though I am among people, while in actuality I am still alone. I hear intimate conversations of people passing overhead. I sit in the wet and swampy dark. I like it. I try to build a composite sketch of what a person looks like based on the snatches of conversation.

Once I heard, "She thought he was going to give her a ring for Christmas. He gave her a pair of slippers from China instead." And I created four people in my head. The two who were talking above, a man and a woman whose noses were pointy; the girl waiting for a ring, who wore her hair in a round curl at the bottom—a round curl that sank when she opened the slippers. And the young man. I saw him whistling, oblivious to the world of women and the various things they want.

Jude sometimes comes under the boardwalk with me. I never think there is anything awkward or strange about an older man closing his eyes under the boardwalk with someone my age, but he acts like we have to be careful and sneaky. "Don't ever tell anyone," he says and presses his finger to my lips, removing it before I can open my mouth.

"It's best if you don't peek through the cracks," I tell him. "It's more fun to imagine the people."

"Maybe in your imagination," he says. Still, he tries. He listens. He shuts his eyes. Always at first it is hard to hear people talking over the ocean, especially at night as the waves get louder when it is dark out. Tired long creaks in the boardwalk signal an approach, and with concentration, the voices that pass overhead, become distinct communications. "Like I always say, let peace begin with me." A voice snakes down through the boards.

"See," I say. Jude's eyes are still closed. "You can see that man, crystal clear."

Jude sighs. "Yes. I can. I see how his pants are hitched up higher than most people's."

More voices pass up above. One says, "Something smells funny. Smells like—" but a wave hits the beach and neither of us can hear what word was said, what it was that it smelled like, so the person who said it seems suddenly very mysterious.

Jude keeps his eyes shut. I take the opportunity to stare at him. His lips are very red. Tiny bits of skin are flaking off them. In the light creeping through the boardwalk cracks I see yellow deposits of wax in his ears. This wax intrigues me. It seems so adult, and all the things that make us different make me want him more. A wave crashes on the shore. I wish it were a tidal wave, something strong that would rock me backwards and throw Jude's body on top of mine. I am imagining it so clearly I can feel it when from up above we hear a voice say, "Please, I'm telling you love is a broken-down old car by the side of the road and sometimes you have to rig a fan belt or an alternator with what you've got." A couple breaking up.

I imagine the man who said it looks like Jude though a simpler version of Jude. Like Jude after someone had stood in front of him saying, "Spit it out," as a parent would to a child. Like Jude if someone had said, "Spit it out," to him and he had opened his mouth and out came something as black and green as stomach bile and the something was all the bad things about Jude, everything he had seen in the war in Iraq, everything that made him so melancholy. The man on the boardwalk sounds like Jude if Jude had then run down to the ocean and washed the bad parts of himself off his hands, off the corners of his lips, rinsed his mouth out with seawater, and as if he'd then stood on the boardwalk as a simpler man, a good man for marrying, saying, "Please, I'm telling you love is a broken-down old car by the side of the road and sometimes you have to rig a fan belt or an alternator with what you've got."

To which I would answer, "Right. Let's get married." But Jude isn't saying that. He is sitting with his eyes closed, saying nothing. "Jude, that's you. He sounds like you."

"Huh." He opens his eyes. "Let's see if we can find him." We roll out from underneath the boardwalk. I laugh loudly to draw attention to us. I think, "I hope everyone sees us coming out from underneath the boardwalk together. I hope they think that Jude and I were kissing underneath there." I think, "Making out." I want them to know he is mine even if it's not true.

Up on the boardwalk we don't find anyone who matches the voice. Jude turns to look at me, shrugs his shoulders, and stares into my eyes long enough that velocity, the force with which a body approaches or recedes from another body, hits me hard. It pushes me towards him by my sternum with everything it has. Jude looks scared and I suppose that is how he should look because the hollow of not having him has given me something powerful to do. He steps backwards.

Some nights I want Jude so badly I imagine I am giving birth to him. I pretend to sweat. I toss and wring my insides out. Mostly I think this because that's how badly I want Jude's head between my legs. It never occurs to me that I imagine he's my baby because loving him hurts or because with the way he drinks, he acts like one. I never think that. Instead I think, I will create Jude inside my head and that way he will be inside of me which is almost as good as fucking or at least pricking our fingers and touching them together.

MAROONED

My room is on the third floor of our house. The house gets thinner towards the top and the staircase that winds its way up to that floor is so narrow and steep, it is more like a ladder than a stair. It has always made me feel cozy, as though I am sleeping curled up in the crow's nest. Our house was once apartments for sailors so it is broken up oddly. I have my own bathtub up on the third floor. There is a window over my tub and when I was younger, I'd lie down in the tub instead of my bed. My mother would wake me and make me move back to my bed but finally she gave up and let me sleep there. I liked it in the tub because from the window I could see stars and the ocean and sometimes, if it was calm, I could see the stars in the ocean. I liked the tub because if I slept with my ear against the drainpipe I could hear my parent's conversations all night long, metallic talking that made its way up through the plumbing.

Through the pipe, one night just before my father disappeared, I heard him tell my mother, "I remember how the moon shines into the ocean and the pattern it makes on the sea floor." She didn't say anything. "I want to go back there," he said, and the reason I remember that conversation is because my mother started crying when he said that and I had never heard her cry before.

He meant we were from the ocean. "You're a mermaid," he told me at the breakfast table. "Don't forget it." A corner of toast scraped the roof of my mouth when he said it. The cut it made helped me to remember. So I don't think he's dead. I think he is in the sea swimming and that is kinder than imagining his boots filling up with water, and then his lungs.

People often suggest that it would be better if we knew for certain whether or not my father is dead. That, to me, seems cruel, as if they want me to abandon all hope. That's how dreary people try to keep things here on dry land.

Despite them, I remain hopeful. Even though my father is becoming more like a page of paper that yellows with time, or the way a dream slips ahead of the waking dreamer, or the way people get hard-skinned with age and use that hard skin like a file to toughen up their children.

Am I a mermaid? I once was certain. But now, the older I get, the vaguer things become.

My father has been gone a long time, eleven years. Still my grandfather, mother, and I keep a lazy vigil, if that combination of words is possible, lazy + vigil. We watch for him, even in the winter though we are so far north that sometimes the ocean freezes. It is dangerous. Icebergs as big as boulders form. If my father decided to return in the winter he might get crushed by the ice. We don't move away from this small town because we are waiting for him to return.

My father's parents used to work as typesetters until the press closed down. My grandfather lost his job, and my grandmother, an immigrant from France named Marcella, died. The press was called the Constantinople Press because they made maps and books about maps and dictionaries about maps. My grandparents were responsible for breaking up printed plates of type into letters again, filing fonts—Caslon with Caslon, Bernhard with Bernhard, Times with Times—and the broken type went into a device called the hellbox, a very hot cabinet where the letters got melted down to lead and readied for recasting.

The press was loud. The workers there communicated by using plates of letters to write quick notes to one another. That is how my grandfather wooed my grandmother. He would send her plates of type that he had written just for her.

—Ma Fluer
Each clang! clang! clang! of the press is a
sweet message whispered in your ear from
me, saying Love! Love! Love!

My grandmother fell in love with my grandfather in backwards words. So that now, even though the Constantinople Press has closed, my grandfather continues to set type into a dictionary he is writing. It gives him something to do and it reminds him of her.

I think my grandfather fell in love with her for the way she spoke. In America, her French began to wither. Her English was slow and clunky, marked by confusions.

> **bridal–adj.** of or relating to a bride or a marriage
> ceremony.

> **bridle–n.** a harness, consisting of a headstall, bit,
> and reins, fitted about an animal's head and used
> to restrain or guide the beast.

My grandmother had come to the United States during World War II because the town where she had grown up was first destroyed by the Nazis on their charge into Paris.

Then it was destroyed and finally toppled—the fields ruined, the houses burned, and the people killed—as the
Allies beat the Nazis into their retreat. She was sixteen
and orphaned. She sailed to America on a ship named
the *Mirabella*. She liked the ship because she thought its
name was close to hers, Marcella. She thought that was
a sign from her dead parents. She told me she also liked
the ship because, "It was filled with doors," and that to
her seemed like a chance to change. But when she arrived
in America she didn't change at all. She chose this town
because it looked like her own town in France: small and
cramped. If you can trace a characteristic—curved finger-
nails or pointy canines or alcoholism—back to one ances-
tor, I can trace my hatred of the dry land back to her. She
had more reasons than anyone to hate the dry land, having lived through a war that she had nothing to do with.

Our house is still divided into sailors' apartments. We just
keep all the doors open in between the different apartments so that it seems more house-like. In this way our
house resembles a tremendous heart, one with sixteen
chambers. We have many rooms that have become ware-
houses for the junk my mother collects or items neither
she nor my grandfather can bear getting rid of. In the
different rooms we keep my grandfather's drawers of lead
type, cardboard files of pretty pictures that my mother has
torn from magazines, the contents of my grandmother's

house, including a yellow velvet loveseat with lion's paws for feet and an armoire that still holds the baby clothes for a child my mother miscarried, and almost every toothbrush my family has used since we moved into this house the year before I was born. Our dining room has stacked empty frames leaning against the available wall space. They are twenty-five deep in places, and my mother hopes to use them one day. Underneath the kitchen sink there used to be a box where we kept spent lightbulbs until my mother decided to store coffee cans there instead. I don't know what happened to the dead lightbulbs. We have three sewing machines and four typewriters because my grandfather buys cheap ones from the classified section in the weekly newspaper. All seven bedrooms have beds because once my mother thought she could open the house up as a bed and breakfast. It didn't work out, so now all the extra beds that are not in use are covered: one with contour maps of the islands off the coast where we live; some with my grandmother's records, mostly opera and European folk songs. The other beds are covered with books.

Still somehow I manage to walk through our house and think that we aren't trash.

We have so many rugs that in the living room we have spread them out on top of each other. We have two pianos even though my mother is the only one who knows how to play. The saddest thing we've held onto is my father's wing chair. It is frightening because the upholstery is still stained from his hand oil and he has been gone for so many years. In the kitchen we keep the china from both my mother's and grandfather's weddings, a set of Stangl Ware, and an ever-expanding set of daily ware that we acquire one piece at a time when we shop at the A&P Superstore. There are two rooms used as libraries, for which my mother and grandfather keep two separate and opposing systems of organization in their heads— hers by subject, his by the way he feels about the author: **A**nimosity, **B**etrayed, **C**urious, **D**elighted, etc. Piles block other piles. Once a neighbor's young child had his arm broken there when a stack of books gave way.

Despite all the evidence in the house of objects sur- viving the people who once owned them, my mother and grandfather agree that if they hold on to everything their chances of surviving are better. I don't subscribe to this line of thinking, though I can imagine one situation where all the debris in our house could be useful. That is when the ice caps are done melting and our house is underwater, then I could see my grandfather and my mother fashioning a raft out of what they once owned, a couch or a table, and climbing aboard, paddling the raft towards the Rocky Mountains and away from the incoming tide.

I keep my room mostly empty except for a bed, a dresser, and a few pictures on the wall. One picture is of a polar ex- plorer who, during World War I, left Elephant Island on a far smaller boat than the boat he'd arrived on. The picture is tattered but I like it because the explorer was so brave. He left his marooned crew behind where their ship had been frozen solid, stuck in the pack ice. In a small launch he went for a rescue. He sailed into a cove on South Georgia Island in the Antarctic where he ate some albatross meat after not having eaten meat in a long time. He crossed a highly crevassed and dangerous glacier with brass screws taken from his launch fixed to the soles of his shoes so he'd not slip on the ice. Though he still did slip. In thirty-six hours he covered only forty miles. After the first hour or two his brain began to repeat words in the same patterned battering his boat had suffered. Oddly, he felt that the words did not grow out of him but came from some exterior source. The words were, "The girl who sold seashells will someday rot in hell. The girl who sold seashells will someday rot in hell." The words repeated and repeated until their stresses were highly over-accentuated and he could not stop and in fact found himself marching across the crevassed tundra in time to the pounding of the words.

I like the picture because it is the same with me only the words are, "He loves me not. He loves me not. He loves me not." I don't mean God or my father. I mean Jude the sailor, the mortal I love.

LETTING GO OF RED

Jude came home from the war in Iraq a year and a half after the president had declared the war was over. He wasn't even supposed to be there at all. He'd already served three years and seven months of his term, but when the war started he decided to stay on for a bit. He needed the money. He doesn't own a fishing boat and so he didn't have much choice as there is almost no other way for men to make money here.

When he finally got home we took a walk out on the small part of the bay that freezes every year. Since I was older than when he had left and had been pining for him the entire time he was gone, writing him love letters every single week, I thought that the purpose of the walk would be that he was finally planning on collapsing on the ground before me, planning to bring his lips to my winter boots and make out with them, writhing with love. This however turned out not to be the purpose of the walk. Jude was war-torn. He was distracted and I found that I had to make eye contact with him before I started talking or else he might not realize that I was speaking to him. Since he got home he'd been drinking a lot and taking some pills that an Army social worker had gotten for him when he was still enlisted. I was frustrated as he'd been gone a year and a half and there were lots of things I wanted to tell him and this made it hard. "Jude." Wait for eye contact. He looks. Continue talking. "When you were gone the bay didn't freeze and they said it was because of global warming but I don't think so. I think it was because I'd come down here looking across the ocean to see where you went. I kept the ocean warm loving you. Can you imagine what—" A bird flew overhead and Jude turned his attention away. I lost him.

"I want to move to Mexico," he said. "Or Canada. I don't care which one."

"Why? You didn't kill anybody, right?"

A fisherman had cut a circular hole in the ice and we stood on either side. Jude reached down through the hole. He didn't answer. "I went to the Middle East on board a supply ship that was carrying some Bradley fighting vehicles and some other shit. There were these holding stations in the bottom of the ship that were five stories below the surface of the ocean. There was a strange pressure on your brain down there."

"Like the bends?"

"Like the pressure of a ship full of supplies and soldiers who are off to war and are too scared to speak and so start screaming at the ocean after days out at sea. Down in the hold, the screams echo. I swear to God, the hold holds onto the yelling and bounces it around."

Jude didn't go to Mexico and he didn't go to Canada. Instead he tore up his Social Security card while I watched. He thought that was a good idea until he was denied military disability because his body wasn't wounded, just his head. So he went down to the welfare office to apply, but the first document they wanted to see from him was his Social Security card. So Jude gave up on the government.

When Jude got home from Iraq he went back to his old job fishing. It doesn't pay well but it does pay him in cash at the end of each day depending on what is caught. It's what he used to do before he joined the Army. He's good at it, but if you don't own your own boat it's a very hard way to live.

"I already served my four years so I thought about deserting. I didn't want to kill other poor people. I didn't want anything to do with the war anymore. But if you desert, the Army hires brutal guys who hunt you down and turn in AWOL soldiers for money. They throw you in a military prison that would make a regular prison look like a resort. You have no rights and the people guarding you are other soldiers so they really want to kill you for deserting. I didn't have the spine for it but I thought about it every day."

Even though Jude is back from the war he still is not my boyfriend the way I thought he would be. But he stays close by and he takes care of me. When I need it, he'll shake my hand with a twenty dollar bill folded up inside his palm. He passes me the money, smiling like he's a big-time crime boss or like he's my father. When I come down to the docks to meet his boat he stands directly behind me, his shoulder and thigh touching mine so that an ex-con named Larry, who was sent to prison for arson though every one knows he also killed his girlfriend, will stop leering the way he does at anything female. Jude and I see each other every day. Last week he brought me a miniature bouquet, like a bouquet for a mouse. It was one or two purple asters, their stems wrapped in the foil from a peppermint patty. Sometimes he comes by after noon, after the boat he fishes for gets in, or else he'll drop by before he goes out drinking or sometimes if he's feeling badly he'll make a howling sound, a coyote noise, late, late at night outside my window. I'll look down into the street at him and when he sees me he stops howling and just looks at me until he calms down. We don't talk but stare at each other through the glass of the window. After fifteen minutes or so he usually goes home to bed.

Jude is in my kitchen watching me get lunch for my grandfather, a tin of tuna fish with some crackers soaked in the fish-packing oil. My grandfather is in the living room typesetting his dictionary, like a crossword puzzle but a bit more involved. He is working on the etymology of the word "hold," as in a ship's hold. He'll go back centuries, looking through old dictionaries, cross-referencing any usage, searching for the word's birth. When I bring him his lunch I ask, "What have you found?"

"Well, the word *hold* is Dutch in origin. It's actually *hol* and shares a root with *hollow*."

"That's nice." Jude is sitting on our kitchen stool with his legs gently parted.

"But even closer in origin," my grandfather continues, taking a bite of the tuna fish, "is the word *hell*."

I pass Jude in the kitchen and I can smell him. He has been drinking. Still he smells good. "Come here, girl," he says and pulls me towards him so that I can feel his breath on my neck. Jude and I do not have any regular sort of relationship. He is not my boyfriend. He says he is too old to be my boyfriend. But he pulls me onto his lap. He breathes in my ear. He has never kissed me despite his kissing most girls who live here, this far north. Jude thinks he is too old for me. I think I could cut a strip of flesh from his upper arm and eat it.

"You smell like 3-in-One," he tells me.

I think that is a compliment until I realize he means the appliance oil. I think on it a bit longer and open my neck up, 3-in-One. He *holds* me. He *hollows* me. He *hells* me.

He doesn't talk about the women he goes out with and when I ask him he says, "But that's got nothing to do with you and me." That's not the way I see it, and so eventually Jude gets drunk and then I ask him and then he tells me everything, not just about the women but everything. "We did it in the basement of the ironworks," he'll say, or, "You know her husband doesn't care what she does at night," or, "Those cuts on my ribs are because I am trying to open gills before the flood comes." So he doesn't really have any secrets and he doesn't really have any gills because where he cut himself scarred up with thick, white, foamy tissue and nobody could breathe through that.

Twice since he's been back I have seen Jude walking with women who I know are his girlfriends. Once I saw Jude and a woman waiting outside the SeaScrubbers Laundromat. It was cold out but the woman and Jude stood outside. The woman was standing behind Jude and using her fingers like a comb through his hair. I watched for as long as I could until I began to imagine that she was yanking his hair out in clumps and dropping it on the sidewalk that was already filthy with dryer lint. I was so mad. I realized that if she actually did yank out Jude's hair it would make me happy, so I walked away. The second time I saw him with another woman, it was a different woman. I remember this one because Jude was sitting with her in the Reach Road Restaurant and they were sitting on the same side of a booth. The other bench was just empty, like they didn't care what other people thought.

When I see him walking with women that I don't know I feel how I am not a part of this town. I feel as though I were floating in the surf and saw him on dry land with another woman but when I swim to shore I realize too late that I don't have legs but a big tail and then I am beached and suffocating and the people who live in town are poking me with a stick wondering, "What the hell is she?" I can't breathe. When I see Jude with women that I don't know I feel like my eyes are suffocating me. What I see is choking me. Jude's girlfriends hurt me. They take my breath away and leave a mark like the bright-blue residue on my eyes after flash photography. In the moment that I stop breathing the picture of whatever burned me becomes trapped. I'll see a blue afterimage and it looks like Jude in a cheap bar with a woman cheaper than me.

I asked an ophthalmologist for help. He comes to town once a month, like the full moon. He is part of a traveling medical clinic paid for by the state for poor people. I thought that because of this he was probably stretched too thin. I worried he wouldn't grasp the subtleties of my problem. When I called to make the appointment a tired nurse inquired, "Well, what seems to be the problem?" So I told her I was in love so badly that it was affecting my vision.

"Are you wasting my time?" she asked.

"No, Miss." I realized too late that I should have said Ma'am instead of Miss.

"Well the doctor's got an opening next Tuesday. Come then."

On Tuesday there is a selection of old magazines in the state's waiting room. Some are catalogs, some are for horse owners or women or amateur photographers or doctors and medical students. I take one of these with me into Examination Room B. After five minutes or so the doctor enters. He switches on a very narrow piercing light for looking into eyes. He asks, "Well, what seems to be the problem?" So I tell him.

"I am in love and it is affecting my vision." He looks to the left. He looks to the right. He clears his throat. He steps outside the examining room to perhaps consult a medical journal. He takes the opportunity to visit the patient in Examination Room A. I pick up the magazine where I left off. Inside, there is a story of an overweight hemophiliac and the danger his own weight poses. The hemophiliac bleeds without ever breaking his skin, bruises that slip loose and navigate between his skin and his flesh as though through the Erie Canal at night.

The article is breathtaking and so I see a blue after-image of it crawl across the leather case of lenses. In ten minutes the doctor returns. I ask him, "Doctor, how is a hemophiliac like blue?"

He looks extremely puzzled. "Look, I'm an ophthalmologist," he says.

It is easy. Neither can stop letting go of red.

"We'll just keep an eye on this situation," he says. "See me in a month. My girl will make an appointment for you."

I think the trouble with my eyes started because they don't have enough pigment. They are no more colorful than ice with a little blue in them. Eyes are an exception to ocean, sky, and blood. Eyes can be blue where there is oxygen. That is a theory concerning my condition that I have yet to discuss with my ophthalmologist.

ROGUES

The Seas, a motel where I sometimes chambermaid, sits a bit higher than the other motels so that its broad and weathered sign dominates much of its landscape. This motel is not popular with tourists because the largeness of its sign seems desperate.

The woman who owns the Seas named the rooms after different famous hurricanes and leaves cards in each room to describe the storm. It is creepy. So even if a French-Canadian couple wound up at the motel accidentally, chances are they would find it weird and not return the following summer.

The woman who owns the motel could sleep in a different room every night if she wanted to, but usually she stays close to Andrew or the Galveston Hurricane. That way, she told me, if the office phone rings she can hear the answering machine pick up through the walls. So much stillness in the day, she sits on the curb outside the line of empty rooms. She smokes. She's not very old but the cigarettes help her to feel like she is.

She is gloomy like that because both her brother and her father were tuna fishermen who never came back. "They weren't even on the same vessel," she tells me while I am roller-brooming a room, Hugo, and she is smoking, watching me sweep. "But it was one of those storms where a hole opens up in the ocean and seven vessels were lost in one day."

"Hmm," I say and continue cleaning.

"Why do you think the ocean would do that?" she asks.

"Well," I pull out some science. "I think that it has to do with wind speed, fetch, and the curvature of the globe," I say. She looks at me as though I had just dumped a pile of insult onto the carpeted floor I am cleaning and rubbed it in good with the heel of my shoe. I stop roller-sweeping. "Why? Why do you think the ocean would do that?"

She has some more of her cigarette, "I always thought it was because the ocean is like a one-of-a-kind thing, like there is nothing else similar to it in the entire world and so the ocean feels no love, no mother, no father or husband, like a space alien. I always thought that just made it an extremely nasty and greedy thing, like an only child."

"Hmm," I say and nothing else. I am an only child but I need my job so I keep my mouth shut.

There is a lot of this kind of sadness here. It slips in like the fog at night. The fog that creeps out of the ocean to survey the land that one day she thinks will eventually be hers.

Later, after I get home from work, my mother wants to know what I am doing since it is Saturday night and I am a young woman. If she pesters me and makes me go out, I'll go to Jude's. He has an old stethoscope. I'll listen to his heart through his shirt so his scars of gill-cutting don't show. I'll close the bathroom door though not all the way. I'll lift my shirt. Jude will peek through the half-closed door. I will listen to my own heart. Then I'll hold the stethoscope above the mold in the shower and it will say, "We never would have left the ocean had we known what a horrible place this is." And I'll say, "Me too."

After the woman who owns the Seas asked me about why the ocean would make such a storm that both her father and brother would die in it, I asked Jude about it. He didn't know why exactly but he said that on the surface of the ocean, the tallest theoretical wave made by the wind could reach a height of one hundred and ninety-eight feet. This would be called a rogue, any wave over seventy feet is called that. He told me little is known of these waves because if you see one you most often die. These rogue waves usually come in threes. The three sisters is what they are called. Just like the dry land to name the cruel things in the water after women.

The man who traversed the crevassed glacier with brass tacks in his shoes, the man whose picture is tacked to my wall, had arrived at Elephant Island in nothing more than a large launch. He'd left most of his shipwrecked men behind when he went for help. In the launch he saw one of these rogue waves, but because of its height and absolutely straight-up slope it did not make him think of water. The man pointed to the foaming crest of the wave rising above him and said to his crew, "Look at that strange cloud." That is how tall the wave was. He, somehow, lived though that wave.

A rogue wave would stick out like this: Imagine you are reading a book and have arrived at a certain page, but imagine that when you arrived at that page, instead of being five inches wide it is one hundred and ninety-eight feet wide. So wide that when you turn the page it crushes you, pins you underneath it. You would never make it to page 53.

THE SURRENDER PLACES

My mother is a small woman, five two. She is strong but her bones are tiny, and sometimes when I hug her I can feel her heart beat through her chest like the battering of an insect trapped in a lamp.

This town goes to bed very early but my mother does not. She doesn't sleep well without my father and so she avoids sleep or she fakes it. She likes the town better at night. She likes things to be quiet. It is what she is used to.

There is a school on an island just off the coast a few hours south of here. It is a school for deaf children and, outside of the school's building, there is nothing on the island but the founder's pet cemetery. Horses, dogs, birds, and cats mostly. My mother grew up on this island. Both of her parents were deaf. Her father was the Plant and

Property Man responsible for haying a small meadow, shoveling snow, mulching trees, repairing busted desks, washing the chalkboards at night, replacing rotten stairs and broken windows. My mother's mother worked in administration typing health records, report cards, annual budgets in triplicate, and, twice, certified depositions on the accidental deaths of two children enrolled in the school, one drowned, one jumped.

Of the fifty to sixty people who lived on the island there were very few people who could hear things. My mother was one of them. She loved living on the island. She liked not talking and was annoyed that her parents sent her on a ferry every morning to a school for hearing people.

One surprising thing she told me about life on the island was that deaf people are actually very loud, especially deaf children. The reason is because they cannot hear to gauge the volume of their guttural emissions or excited shrieks. In fact my mother says she grew up accustomed to hearing her parents have sex because neither of them could hear the mighty creak their bed made and she was too embarrassed to tell them. So my mother was one of the few people on the island who could hear foghorns at night and seagulls in the morning, and being responsible for so much listening made her a very quiet person.

On the island my mother had a best friend named Marie. Marie was a very good lip-reader because Marie had not been born deaf but lost her hearing swimming in a quarry that, after years, had filled with rain. Something was living in the water, Marie had told my mom, and whatever it was filled her ears and ruined her hearing with an infection. So Marie could talk a little bit, though my mother said Marie sounded like a donkey when she spoke. They'd run to the pet cemetery, and my mother couldn't help but think that the animals were probably pricking up their ears down in their graves thinking that Marie was talking to them. She told Marie her theory. Marie brayed even louder. She wasn't one to get offended because she sounded like a donkey. After that, the two of them always had it in their heads that they could talk to animals, even dead ones, and that was how they enjoyed themselves on the island.

More from Marie than from her parents, my mother tried to get to the heart of what it was like not to hear anything. She was trying to decide whether or not she wanted to be deaf herself. Marie signed to my mother that it wasn't like what she might think. It wasn't like a blank sheet of white paper because actually she heard things all the time. The sounds just came from inside rather than outside, like reading. But then that's not really hearing, my mother answered, and Marie signed that what she meant was that deafness does not equal silence, which my mother understood. She liked to read a lot. Almost constantly. Then Marie said, braying in her way, "Also, it is wonderful."

"It is?"

Marie read my mother's lips and nodded yes.

"Why?"

"I can't tell you. You have to be deaf to understand."

"Give it to me," my mother signed and put her ear up against Marie's ear. They lifted their hats against the cold and aligned their heads like spoons. The cartilage of both their small ears was as plastic as suction cups and after making adjustments they created a tight seal like kissing lips between their ears. Marie closed her eyes, telling whatever deafened her that it was wanted next door and furthermore she didn't want it. It wasn't that wonderful at all. They stood that way, ear to ear both wishing something would happen. They stood that way long enough to convince themselves that this transfer wasn't going to work, and then they were cold and walked back to the school and my mother heard the waves striking against the wooden pylons of their pier and Marie didn't.

"After that, at night I would think about deafness in the way you might think of a beautiful man," she told me. "I imagined its pockets and curves as though I could run my hand across deafness. I thought of it as a dark, heavy blanket that would pin me underneath it while I squirmed, which, at that time," she said and winked, "was exactly what I was looking for."

When her parents retired they moved back here, back to where my mother's father had been born. Immediately my mother stood out as an oddball, a loner, a reader, a young woman who didn't yell at her parents or carry on much. She thought she wanted to be a writer. She thought that she would one day move to New York City and pursue a career.

When she met my father she was still really good at being quiet. When she met him she realized how she had been collecting silence in a slender, delicate glass jar behind her ribcage. The bottle was not corked and so she always had to be very careful not to spill it. When she met him what happened was he took her out dancing and told her, "You make me feel like a pony." She didn't know what the hell that meant, but it made her damp inside like a flood, so the bottle broke and she didn't care anymore as long as she could have him. All the good silent things she'd been saving up, like lights off in the distance at night or fog in the morning, ricocheted around her insides freed and she'd never felt so good. She went wild for him, taking on his habits, like drinking, driving with only one hand on the wheel, and other dangerous interests, as though they were a new coat cut just for her. She tore about town like a match that had just realized it could burn down the entire village if it wanted to, and she did.

Then I came along and soon all her ideas about writing and New York got away from her. My mother told me she would say, "Shhh," and rest her head on my chest listening for my heart to beat or for my stomach to digest.

"I didn't want to be deaf anymore. I didn't even want to be a writer anymore," she told me. "In fact, I realized that the whole deaf/writer thing was just a place to hold the want I had had. This was what I had really wanted. A man to climb up on top of me and a baby to come out."

It's funny that she grew up not talking because now when she speaks she says things like this that other people might not say. It's funny to hear her tell stories about how much she loved me as a baby because I think it has gotten harder for her to love me the older I get.

"You two saved me from a lonely, quiet life. You rescued me."

But I say, "You're the one who pulled me from the water." And so she looks at me sideways again, tired by the way teenagers can lose their minds over things that make no sense to a woman her age.

My mother looks so young that sometimes people mistake us for sisters, but she never tries to fool anyone. She doesn't care if men think she is young or not. She doesn't have much interest in men because she is still in love with my father even though he has been gone for eleven years.

My father was a dark, slender, and quiet man so that when he disappeared it seemed as if he just slipped away, a shard of stone or a splinter of wood. He drank a lot—so did my grandparents, both sets of them—so does most everyone who lives this far north. When my father disappeared I blamed his disappearance on his drinking. I was only eight at the time. Since then I have changed my mind.

Along the shore for hundreds of miles inland the water crops up as lakes and ponds, as if to remind us it was under our feet all the time, traveling through underground tunnels, trying to make its way out to sea. My father told me that when he was young he used to try to make money by cutting blocks of ice from the lakes, storing it in sawdust, and then selling it in the warmer months. His father and his grandfather had always done this for extra cash but my father had a bad time of it, working, as he was, in the time of electric refrigeration. Few people were enticed to buy dirty lake ice when they could go down to the grocery store and get a bag of fresh ice already clean and cubed.

"The lake ice was more beautiful than anything you will ever see. As clear," he said and looked around for an adjective or noun to describe it, but he'd been drinking and the best he could come up with was, "as clear as clear plastic. And," he continued, "huge. Chunks as big as any garbage can or," again he looked around, "as big as the barrel of a man's ribcage. In fact," he told me whispering, leaning forward and tucking his can of beer on the floor beside his armchair, "I traded my ribcage for a chunk of ice instead."

This explained a lot. From my father I got many recessive genes. Fair eyes, fair skin, and the mermaid part.

The surrender places. I did not get a torso of ice, though sometimes it feels that way, as if something solid that once was there melted now and still aches with the vacancy of him when it rains.

I ask my grandfather about the blocks of ice. I'd like to hear him describe the lakes, the ice, the ocean, and how they were when my father was young, but he's a man of few words, with hearing difficulties.

"They melted," he said.

"C'mon."

"There you have your answer," he says, avoiding me, and so I wonder what else he knows but won't say. I wonder if he also feels miles of dark water below him or if what my grandfather feels is just the same old pit of old people and their senility, and he just can't remember how the lakes, the ice, and the ocean used to look because he is old.

My parents captained a boat for my seventh birthday so we could pretend that we lived on an island for the day, and I remember my father saying, "Once when I was gill-netting for a man from Nova Scotia . . ." but then I can't remember the rest of what he said about the man from Nova Scotia. I remember many phrases and sentences my father said to me like, "You let that screen door slam one more time and I'll slam you," or, "When you make Cream of Wheat you have to stir it the entire time or else you get clumps," or, "I wish I'd invented the umbrella," or, "I see your grandmother in you. Open your mouth. Let's have a look. Is she in there?" But these phrases don't even come close to making a complete portrait of him because mostly my father wasn't good at talking. He was far better at sitting silently in his armchair, smoothing the back of his head and then taking a pull off a bottle of beer he kept between his thighs. He'd sit quietly, stirring a mixture of warm water and sugar to nurse back to health a sickly black fly or a disoriented mouse who'd been poisoned by the neighbors. These are the parts of him I find impossible to cut myself loose from. They are beautiful qualities. But beauty is heavy, and though I'm young I am getting tired from carrying around the bits and shreds of my father's beauty.

My mother is still in love with him even though he's been gone eleven years. She says, "Nothing has changed between your father and me. I just don't see him as often." As though he moved to Tallahassee or somewhere else way down south. She'll say something like that and then ask me, "Why do you hang around with Jude? Why don't you go find yourself a nice boyfriend?" But all I have to do is not answer her, and she'll hear how ridiculous that sounds coming from her.

My mother married my father when she was twenty-seven. In those days, this far north, that was old to be getting married for the first time. On their first date my father surprised my mother. Outside the restaurant where they'd eaten he saw something black quickly crawling out of their way. Though he hated to do it, he loved animals, my father leapt, throwing his arm in front of my mother to protect her. With one foot, he squashed the creature. My mother was horrified. "I thought you wouldn't like spiders," he said. But when he lifted his foot it wasn't a spider. It was a cricket.

"Crickets are good luck," she said.

"You are right," he said.

"You killed it," she said, getting to the point quickly the way she does.

"You are right," he said again, shrinking. "I never kill spiders. I love spiders. I did it for you. I thought you might not like them."

"No, I'm not like that," she said. "I love spiders too. I love crickets even more but I love spiders too." Soon after, they were married.

Sometimes if I am soaking in the tub or while I am trying to sleep I picture my father telling me about being a mermaid. I imagine things he might say to me if he were still around. Things like, "You might be living on dry land but you're still subject to our laws," and he'd mean the ocean's laws. I would be relieved to hear this because it would give me comfort. I'd rather be subject to the ocean's laws than the laws that apply to young girls trying to become women here on dry land. For example, many of the carnies at the amusement park are girls I grew up with. One of them has tattooed teardrops on her face, one tear for every year her boyfriend has been in prison. This doesn't strike me as wise, as she is quite young. Though still, sometimes, I secretly wish I had teardrops tattooed on my face, as it seems to give the girl a purpose for now. When you are young, living in the North, sadness can make you feel like you have something to do. Sadness can be like a political cause, almost, or a religion or a drug habit. It is a lot of work to stay sad. I think of the carny girl's teardrops and I can't believe that is her purpose, but still I want a purpose so badly that I am envious even of that sad and ugly purpose she has. I suspect that she wants her boyfriend to stay in prison for a long time so that every year she can add another drop until they reach below the collar of her shirt and everyone who sees her will say, "My. There's a sad girl." She's like an animal with her foot caught in a trap. In the wave of pain that rushes over her, she looks to the sky and she is braced by the color blue there. For a moment she imagines she can escape this ugly town and her imprisoned boyfriend, so she tries to use a knife on her bone above her ankle to free herself from the trap. Sadly, the knives they give out as amusement park prizes here don't have the blade for any real cutting, and anyway she doesn't have the money to move away.

KINGDOM

Sometimes I spend dusk driving around town. Dusk is depressing and I feel the only way I can get warm at dusk is with the car heater blowing directly on me, or if I take a hot bath, but if I take too many baths in one day my mother will become nervous. She'll imagine that I am doing secret things in the bathtub, things like masturbating or killing myself.

Even if Jude's not with me I talk to him. I pretend he is in love with me. "I'll be cheap, Jude," I tell him when he's not there. He meets women employed by the ironworks or he meets girls on the street or in minimarts or they just get into his car if he looks at them. I suppose he is that handsome. That could actually happen. He doesn't always tell me. Sometimes I find their clothes. Sometimes I find their pictures. Sometimes in the pictures they are smiling at Jude. I look until I think I will be sick or until he finds me and says, "Ah, come on. What are you looking at that for? Come here. I got something for you today," and he'll smile. "Come here," and he'll lead me out onto his back concrete stoop and point down into a plastic bucket sitting there. "It's a baby," he'll say, and it is. A tiny baby sea urchin the size of a quarter, covered everywhere with black spines. It is hard to believe something that small is alive.

"That's adorable," I say, and Jude blushes. "Thanks," I say, and kiss his cheek with dry lips. I carry my baby home in a bucket.

I try to meet other men but it doesn't work for me. I get in my car and drive out to the ironworks but the men change shifts. They look at me sideways because I have always been an outcast here. That is what happens to children who lose a parent. They think I am weird or special or unlucky or just too sad a puddle for them to dip their toes into. So the men at the ironworks look at me and even if they notice that I have come of age, they still get into their own cars and go home. I linger long at stop signs in town but no one ever gets into my car even though all the doors are unlocked.

I develop a plan to make Jude jealous, but in order to go through with a plan I have to call a man named Neil I know, though not very well. Jude knows him too because the man is the same age as Jude and sometimes they work for the same captains. That is part of my plan. The man and I decide to have dinner together and hear some music in a town an hour west of here. He doesn't want to go out in our own town. I drive and after dinner, when I return from the ladies room, he says, "Pay the tip." So I do and thank him for dinner. "I'm not taking you out," he says. "You still owe me half." This man Neil is an ugly man, and as the evening passes I begin to see how he enjoys humiliating me. He spends the entire evening talking about a girlfriend he once had from California. When I say, "Oh, the Pacific," he looks at me crossways. "You're a real nut job. Has anyone ever told you that?" I don't like this man. His thick lips make me feel sick inside, but I have a plan so I go though with it and later that night the man Neil says, "I like a lot of talk while we're doing it." I think of all the unleashed dogs on the streets. Their conversations in howl. "So that's what a nineteen-year-old feels like," he says, and I try to imagine the dark words he'll use to describe this to the sailors he works with, to Jude.

Still later, the ceiling in his bedroom.

The hair on the man's back.

Jude is very mad about the man. He says he doesn't want to see me.

I say I am having trouble seeing him too. "I have to go to the eye doctor again," I tell him, but he has already hung up the phone.

A number of weeks pass. I don't see Jude. I work a few days at the sardine factory and a few days as a chambermaid. I spend one day watching a square patch of sunlight travel all the way across my room. I am in misery. Without Jude I have nothing to do. Finally the eye doctor returns.

At his office a small albino boy waits in the front room. He doesn't read a magazine so I assume his pink eyes are blind and I stare at him with no regard for manners. Eventually he says, "I can see you, you jerk."

"Sorry," I tell him, but the boy won't talk to me.

The doctor calls me in. He asks me, "What do you see?" with his hand over one of my eyes.

"Jude."

"Now the other?"

"Jude."

"I see. Not much change. Well, at least it's slow-moving." I think of the patch of sunlight. "We'll keep an eye on it," he says.

I drive to Jude's but I don't go inside. Instead I look at myself in the rearview mirror, looking for whatever it is that deforms me to unlovable—slime or freckles or a tail. I stare and stare. I ruminate, as my mother would say, to the point of destruction, thinking so hard that it feels like drilling. Indeed, I've often imagined performing a dissection on myself so that I could better understand what's going on inside me, but I am too scared to go through with it. Instead I stare in the rearview. Eventually after so much staring I say, "I can see you, you jerk."

I park and walk down to the water. I walk along the shore a long, good distance. There are no people on the beach this far from town. I walk even farther, over the rocks, so I can be all alone and away from my bad decisions. I think of the man Neil and find it impossible to believe that I let him inside of me. I think of Jude and worry that all the mermaid stories are true, that if he won't love me, either he'll have to die or else I will. I think of my father and I stop walking. I take all three of them, the hairy man, Jude, and my father, I ball them up and toss them over my shoulder. I keep walking away from them and, for a minute, I even run along the shore feeling light and lifted. I put one hand on my hip and one hand on the back of my head like a pin-up girl from a 1950s calendar. I swish my hips. Woo woo. Very sexy. After some deliberations I decide to leap. Ready, I prepare myself, start to run and launch into the air. It feels wonderful but halfway through the leap I get scared. I see something squirming up ahead and immediately long to be back on the sand. I abort my leap. I fall back to the ground. There is a creature flapping like a fish without air, only it is far larger than any fish. I run to find out what the thing is, and as I approach I can see that it is not really a fish. It is King Neptune on the shore. He is hurt. He is squirming, trying to get back into the ocean. I am scared but I ask him, "King, do you want me to throw you back?"

"Oh, dear. If you could," he says.

I edge up to him slowly. I don't want to alarm him any further. I am surprised that someone as powerful as King Neptune could be hung up by something as shifting and dirty as a beach. "What happened?" I ask, while trying to lift his back.

"It's embarrassing," he says.

"You don't have to say if you don't want to. You are the king of the ocean." He is a tremendous creature, like a whale. So large I could be crushed if a wave rolled him onto me. I am getting quite wet in my efforts to assist the King.

"No. It's all right. I'll tell you," he says. "Broken heart." King Neptune uses his arms to push toward the water. "There was a young girl," he says. "Here, on the beach. I wanted to get closer to her. But as soon as I came in to the shallow water she stood up and ran away."

"I'm sorry. That's sad." I don't really think it is that sad. I wonder what an old man was doing chasing a young girl but I don't say anything. "Do you know my father?" I ask him.

"What? A sailor?"

"Yes."

"Sorry," he says.

"No. It's not your fault."

King Neptune smiles like God. Like ninety-seven percent of the world's water is in ocean. Like seventy-five percent of the world is covered with ocean. Like everything is his fault.

"What about Jude? Do you know him? He's down here a lot," I say.

"Yeah. I think so. He's friends with that girl who has lost her mind? The one who thinks she's a mermaid?"

I stop helping King Neptune get back into the water. I stand back from him while he continues talking. "What I can't figure out," he says, "is why she'd want to be a mermaid. All mermaids do is swim around and kill sailors. It's not a great job."

I stop helping him and when I start again I push hard. "I'm going to be a different kind of mermaid," I tell the King.

He turns and looks at me. His eyes are just as pale as mine. "You don't get a choice," he says. "There's only one kind of mermaid," he says, and then, "Don't forget that the ocean is full of everything except mercy."

I shove his back so that he'll awkwardly be forced to bend at the hips. He is an old man and I am certain that he won't have the flexibility in his bones, that it will hurt him. I push so hard that the vertebrae in his back cut me.

Fuck King Neptune, I think, because growing up as a mermaid was a hard way to grow. When I was younger, other children would not befriend me, but instead they would say loud enough for me to hear, "That house, that house is rotten in and out. That girl, that girl's got bugs in her hair." I'd fake to pick a bug from my scalp and eat it. Delicious. When I was younger I'd go down to the water and each wave would ask in a thug accent, "You want I should take care of those kids? You want I should tell your father?"

But I'd let the children live. See, I have mercy.

I push and push King Neptune and then I give up. And then I can see clearly. King Neptune isn't, and underneath my cut hands is a rock shaped like a king, a rock deposited on this beach when the ice age flowed home, beaten, in retreat.

FOR REFERENCE

The beach where the sea channel opens into the salt marsh is usually less crowded because the smell of sulfur can be strong when there is no wind. The mouth of the channel expands in a tongue so that it is uncrossable and children have drowned trying.

Jude has brought three blankets, and at the edge of the dune he uses one and a few pieces of driftwood to make us a tent. Jude has forgiven me. He didn't have much choice. Neither one of us really has any other friends.

I fold my pants and sit cross-legged back down on the sand with a deep curve in my shoulders. I watch him unfurl the blanket. I am worn out by desire for him like a girl in some book.

He removes his shirt but sits directly in front of me tucking his arms across his chest because of his weird scars there, scars that look like someone once tried to write Jude a message on his torso with a razor blade, but then changed his or her mind and scribbled the letters out instead. They don't look like gills. Jude resembles a very unhealthy version of Snow White, with black hair and red lips, like a Snow White after years spent drinking in bars. I put my toes on his back, right where his jeans end and walk each toe, one by one, up his vertebrae, as if he were a bony fish. No one else is on the beach. No one is here to see that he is with me. He could take full advantage of me if he only wanted to. When I sit up, I sit around him, one leg on either side of Jude's. I touch his back with my stomach. I lift my hips until they touch him like I am a barnacle on his back. But after he exhales three times, I can feel it, he stands up and says, "Let's go down to the water." Maybe, I think, he is still angry about Neil.

Even if I added up all the things Jude's name rhymes with and all the words I could spell with the letters of his name it would not measure up to him. A phrase like, "Calm as the bottom of the sea" comes closer. I would be a sloppy typesetter using the more economical "Jude" in lieu of, "Smooth night with stars for navigation."

When I first met Jude he told me my skin was so pale that he thought he could see through it. "You're like the acetate pages of an anatomy book," he said. One page holds blood with oxygen, one page is blood without. "I can see what you had for lunch," he said, and then poked me in the stomach, which made me feel awkward because he is fourteen years older than me and fourteen years younger than my mother, like he is a ball tossed between us. Sometimes he'll be on my side, but sometimes one of them will remind the other of, *And the red bird sings, I'll be blue because you don't want my love.* I've never even heard of that song. But Jude has heard of everything. There is nothing he doesn't have some knowledge of or thoughts on. Having Jude is like having a dictionary the size of a man beside me. I open him up and ask him all sorts of questions.

Until my grandfather finishes his dictionary, which probably won't ever happen, the biggest dictionary in the world will still be the *Oxford English Dictionary*. It's enormous. We don't have one. It's too expensive. Instead we have a condensed OED. The cover is as navy as a bruise. I looked up the word *navy* in it and found that this word shares a history with *nausea* and *navel* from the Sanskrit *na* or *sna* or *snu*, which means to bathe, as in the word *snake*. Unwound language can look like the white cord of unwound brain. It can be dangerous to unwind some words. Jude wasn't in the Navy. He was in the Army and *army* comes from *ar*—to fit, to join, see **art**, see **inertia**, the dictionary says.

When Jude joined the Army he was twenty-six years old. He and two other new recruits spent their first nights away from home in a motel. Their assignment there was indefinite. On the first night Jude climbed up to the roof to see if the ocean was anywhere in sight and to get away from the other new recruits. The other recruits were both bodybuilders. They had a caliper to measure body fat and they seemed anxious to try it out on Jude. They called each other "privates" and laughed.

From the roof Jude saw the two soldiers leave the motel. In the next hour and a half they worked the eastern and the western street corners trying to find a girl who would let them buy her a drink. Jude heard them. He had a good bird's-eye view to watch them after each woman walked away saying, "No, thank you," or saying nothing. The privates would shoot at her, pretending their arms were machine gun arms.

On the roof, Jude said, before bed, he spread his wings and looked toward the edge.

Jude returned to the room not long after the soldiers had gotten in bed. "Where were you all night, man?" they asked.

"Upstairs," he answered.

"Oh yeah?" said one.

"Cause you missed out. We met three squaws and brought them back here."

"Yeah, we waited for you but after awhile we had to plow all three."

"That's right. Here. Here and once on the bed you are now sleeping in, señor."

Jude did not tell them that he knew they were liars but hid it in his chest like a white light that kept him awake through the night. He felt, that very first night, that he had a made a mistake enlisting. He tried to sleep but remembered a bird, a crow he'd found when he was a kid. The bone that kept the crow's wing attached to the crow's body had been popped, and Jude couldn't stand to kill the bird so he left it there. Eventually other animals ate it.

Then, Jude said when he told me about the other new recruits, "I wasn't going to make that mistake again." After the soldiers had fallen asleep Jude stood at the end of their beds, raised his arms like machine gun arms, and fired. See **art**. See **inertia**.

AT JUDE'S HOUSE

Scientists came to where we live to study us because we have the highest rate of alcoholism in the country. Higher, they said, than even the Indian reservations in the West, higher than Florida or Texas or Louisiana or all the other flat states.

The people who lived in Jude's house before Jude did were alcoholics. They used to pour their bacon fat on the carpet in the kitchen just like it was a dirt floor, and where there is not bacon grease from some ancient and filthy breakfast there is the aroma of old cat urinations. Despite these odds Jude tries to make his house pleasant, or he tried to once, and the evidence of this effort is still visible, if barely. For example, he has spread a colorful serape across the back of his couch and tied back the kitchen curtain with a bandanna. He buys a new bath mat whenever the old one gets too dirty. And on the refrigerator he has taped a picture of me from a long time ago, when we first met. You can't tell it's me but it is. You can't tell it's me because I have my back to the camera, bending over the railing of a roadway bridge looking down into the water.

I pass the harbor on the way to Jude's house and see that the boat he has been skippering has come in. It is starting to get dark. That means he is probably home drinking a beer. I scuff the salt and sand on the road while I walk. It makes the rubber soles of my shoes vibrate in a way that runs a tickle up the inside of my leg. I like to go to Jude's house in the afternoon, because when Jude drinks his beer he will usually pat the sofa beside him so I'll come sit down, and he'll say something like, "I've been thinking about the volcanoes on the Pacific Rim," or, "Once I met a man who was a professional card counter in Reno," or, "One night, in a storm so beautiful, I considered jumping overboard," and those are all stories I like to hear. He tells them and he makes the world seem enormous. The stories are a torch he is shoving into the dark corners, pushing the perimeters back farther and farther. It was Jude who told me about the great polar explorer. It was Jude who tore his photo from a magazine and pinned it to my wall so I'd know how big the world is.

A gray sedan filled with three boys and one girl I have known all my life drives past. One boy in the back rolls down his window and screams out to me, "Re, re, re, re, retard!" His stutter is so awful he was held back two grades in elementary school. The car slams on its brakes. I keep walking. It is my habit to ignore the people I have to share this town with. When I arrive at their rear tire, the girl, the driver, her name is Mary, peels out, spitting up road dust all over me so that grains of grit flood my mouth and teeth.

Jude is my only friend here apart from my mother and my grandfather. But Jude is my best friend and no one ever bothers me when I am with him. Still, I must be careful because Jude is two people. He is a tender sailor whose hands seem too rough and large for the delicate way he makes me feel watched over. But he keeps this version of himself locked behind his ribcage until he sees me. The rest of the time he is somebody else. He is a man who lives here and so fills his mouth with all the cheap and garbled words in this town.

I see his house and I start to run. I will tell him about the gray sedan and if I am lucky he will say, "Who was it? I'll fucking kill them," and I will believe him, because once when we were waiting at a traffic light in town with the windows rolled down, some kid in the car next to ours beaned me with an ice cube. It hit me right in the eye and I started screaming. I thought a bird had flown into me.

Jude blocked the car with his truck. He pulled the driver out by his jacket collar and then I stopped looking. I hid my face in my hands. Still I could hear it. It sounded like rotten fruit. When Jude got back in the truck his hands were covered with blood. He didn't say anything and we drove away.

I open Jude's kitchen's screen door and knock on the glass. I can't see all the kitchen, just part of the table and part of the fridge. I cup my hands around my eyes and peer in. It is getting dark and he hasn't turned on his lights yet, but through the doorway I can just make out the kitchen table. There is something wrong with it. It is shaking like a wounded animal or a crippled person. I think Jude is having a heart attack. I walk in. I stand staring, almost excited by the damage we are doing to ourselves. Jude has a woman on his kitchen table. Her skirt is up around her waist and her hair is long and feathered down her bare back. I try to leave but my body is heavy. I stumble so they hear me, and she screams. "Who is she? Who is she?" the woman is yelling while straightening herself up, lowering her hideous skirt. She starts to yell and slap Jude on his arms. He doesn't bother to straighten himself up. I look at Jude and Jude looks at me. That's what's wrong with my eyes.

I turn and run. The drinking-problem scientists are everywhere outside collecting data, leaning against the house, listening through special scientific instruments, jotting notes on clipboards, changing shifts, going on coffee breaks. My eyes are killing me. I have trouble seeing and stumble and scream, "Get your science off me!" but it is just a tree and just its branches. I lean against the tree. I throw up on its roots and rest my head on its bark. I could use something to drink. "I could use something to drink," I scream at the scientists. But there are no scientists, actually.

Jude told me that the polar explorer on my bedroom wall had been stopped by encroaching winter. The expedition was crushed by pack ice. Still, all the sailors survived over three years until their rescue came. They encountered horrors certainly, but perhaps they did not encounter the worst. The worst never has an account because the worst means that you are dead. I am not dead yet, though I feel so bad I might be close. I imagine that even if a sailor lived through the worst storm and spoke to the papers, the sailor might report, "The sea said 'I get you' and did not mean 'get' as in 'understand' like I initially thought." The newspapers would translate what the sailor had said into, "The first wave snapped the pilothouse in two."

The sailor would say, "Yes, the sheer wall of the wave was blue water, but the wall held still for a minute and watched us, gathering strength." And the paper would translate it into, "The first shock of capsizing is the loss of up and then down."

Sailor, "Her skin was so soft I thought I could touch her cold insides." Paper, "One survivor is being held at 18 Winds Sanitarium for rehabilitation and questioning."

Still many people enjoy living by the ocean because it produces gruesome stories exaggerated by gossip, whispers about how in winter it takes 2.5 seconds for a fisherman who has gone overboard hauling a heavy net to die. The water is that cold. Or how four teenagers were bored in March and decided to row out to an island. They could not get back in and had to spend the night in the open boat. In the morning only one girl was still alive so she strangled herself with the towline. Or how a troublemaker was smuggling black powder in his father's boat for money. He blew it up by accident. The skin on his face melted in liquid drips from the fire and froze that way when he gave up the boat and jumped into the water, swimming for the shore and prison. Or how a young woman started her car at the top of a hill. She picked up as much speed as she could and broke through an iron rope fence so she and the car flew out over the cliff and landed three hundred feet below on the rocks, missing the ocean with her bad aim. Or how a man stood beside the water at night and imagined he could walk across the ocean's floor and make his way out to the horizon line. And then he was no longer imagining it but doing it.

Down at the ocean I stare out at the horizon also. I see my grandmother Marcella walking on the line that makes her name. *Mare. Ciel.* Seasky. She is the horizon line. She's as big and bright as a setting sun. I stare at her long enough so that she looks blue in an afterimage on my eye. I burn the sight of her into my pupils, and that way, I can keep her with me for a few burnt hours. "Take these numbers," she says, and passes me a drawerful of lead numbers, depth readings she's stolen from a nautical map. They are mostly shallow numbers. "There," she says. "I removed all warning from the maps. Someone's bound to wreck on the rocks, a sailor, yours, Jude."

JOB

A woman who lives next door asked me to teach her French so she could get a summer job in one of the shops for Canadian tourists. My French is not that good, as I learned it from my grandmother who, by the time I came along, had forgotten a lot of her mother tongue. Still I knew enough to help her a little bit. *Oui! Nous parlons français!*

I told her *voler* oddly enough means both to fly and to steal in French. *Faites attention* those who *voler*. I told her to say, *Nous sommes ouvert demain*. She said, *Nous sommes ouvert deux mains*. Like a dissection. She got the job and when I see her in there she usually comes out to tell me, "Mercy! Mercy!"

I was not baptized until I was eight. All those years, I guess I would have gone to hell if I'd died. Mercy. I considered this and at the ceremony I crossed myself over and over. Finally the quiet priest asked me to stop. He spilled holy water on my dress on purpose.

When we got home my mother apologized for being so tardy with saving my soul. I told her that's OK, since I was a mermaid I didn't have one anyway. My mother gave my father a dirty look, but when she turned away he winked at me quickly. My mother said, "Well still, I'm sorry. It's just that I have trouble with church. All I hear before communion is the congregation coughing and it seems all those germs are collecting in the cup of heaven." She was three months pregnant when I was baptized and she worried about germs. She had reason to worry. She had a stillborn after eight months, and when her water broke the doctors made her deliver the dead baby anyway. She gave birth to a tiny blue girl four months after my father disappeared. In English I said, "She flew away, Mom. Don't be sad." But she said, "Flew? She was stolen. Your father came and took her from us." And my mother doesn't even know how to speak French.

Once I got another job taking care of an older woman. I did it because I had heard that her right foot was flattened like a flipper. I thought that she might be a mermaid too, and I thought it would be a good job because I could ask her questions. I had to help her get into and out of the bath, and on the first day of work she told me, "Nudity is more painful to me than loneliness," as if to explain what was about to happen, as if to explain her defeat in having to hire me. She was propped up against her sink. I was seated on the toilet tank when she said this. Her dress was loose, with two small clasps at the neck which she herself released. Her naked body was horrible, like bulbed growths on trees. Her flipper foot was twice as wide and long as her other foot. The bones in the flipper foot lifted up out of the surface and the deformed skeleton was visible underneath the skin that clung to it. I stared to get used to the foot and the other lumps of her unusual body. I never did get used to her abnormalities, but began to appreciate that perhaps the roundness of her deformities was filled with the collected wonder of views from the cliff, high above where most people lived.

"Did you ever have a husband?" was my first question.

"No. I never married," she said. "Which is probably no surprise. I am not agreeable." I have heard the things people say about mermaids. Jude won't marry me and I'll never be able to kill him, and so I'll never be able to go back to the ocean, and who knows what will happen to me without a husband? My mermaid parts will start creeping out over time, like the woman's sickening foot.

"I've never even had a lover," she said. "Once I wrote a letter to the university requesting a team of scientists make a study of me. However, they did not. I've always thought that was a terrible waste."

She let the water out of the drain herself and stretched her arms towards me, above her, waiting to be picked up.

"Are you a mermaid?" I finally asked her, and she lowered her arms, stared straight ahead at the drain lever, and said nothing, as though she hadn't considered that before and was stumped, or as though that was a sad topic she had almost forgotten and wished I hadn't mentioned it.

My mother works part-time for the public school. There is one deaf child in our town. The school employs my mother as interpreter. Karen, that's the little deaf girl's name, spends a lot of time with my mother outside of school, too, and some days when I find my mother and Karen signing away in our kitchen, sometimes I feel jealous and I make the one sign I know, my middle finger, at Karen behind her back. The public school job does not pay much at all. My mother sometimes works with me chambermaiding at the tourist motels, or we take on shifts at the sardine factory. They call us when they need us. At the factory, by 4 o'clock our hands are silver and slick from scales and soya oil. If I knit my fingers together my hands become odd fish themselves. They even try to swim away but I catch them.

The factory only hires women; even the foreman is a woman. I work at the end of my line, which is fine because the conveyor belt makes it difficult to hear. There is little possibility for conversation. I talk to the fish, "What'd you do last night?" I ask as they fly past on the machinery.

I imagine them swimming in schools, in the deep sea, out for a good time until—swoop—the net closed in. The sardines look up at me with a haughty, empty eye, so I cut their heads off and stuff them into a coated tin. Or else some days, when Jude is on my mind, I can grow inordinately attached to one beautiful sardine. I put it in the front pocket of my apron. Then I grind myself against the conveyor belt, pretending the sardine is Jude. I push it close to me.

The woman who works beside me has been at the factory for thirty-five years. She talks to herself all day long. She has quite a bit to say.

"Mister," I once heard her say, starting a conversation that she continued for the entire eight-hour shift. She played both sides of a conversation. The first role was her, the second role was a very mean man. I couldn't figure him out—he sounded like God or a doctor or a police officer with a sadistic streak. She said, "There's a lawn furniture set at Zayre's."

"And how much is the set?" she, as the man, in a deep voice answered.

"Well, I was hoping you could do something about that because it's more than I've got."

And then, "Woman!" from the mister's side of her conversation, "What'd you spend all your money on?"

And then back to her, "I never actually got any money to spend."

Then him, "Why don't you get a husband first, then a patio set."

"I can't. I'm fifty-five years old. I'm past fresh."

"Woman! Trying to take all my money!"

She stuffed her tin. "No better than the slithery snake that got us here," she said as the mister. And I thought about what was in my apron, the Jude/sardine. I ground it against me and I thought that he, she was right. Those are the choices for women who live here. Dirty. Domesticated. Deaf. Deformed. Slithery. Siren. Psychotic. Silent.

OST OVE

My mother is upstairs looking for something. She is starting to spit words. "Damn. Damn. Where the—" Her search will continue in this vein for a while until she gives up, exhausted. Rarely does she find what she is looking for. The house is just too full to be able to find anything.

My grandfather is working on his dictionary. Often he has to mix and match fonts and sometimes he leaves words out if too many letters are missing. He's talking to himself but I hear him say, "What's lost or love without any Ls?" Ost ove, I think. He tries to work for a bit without any Ls but then he calls out to me. "I think I have a drawer of Palatino in the attic. Would you, dear?"

"Please no," I say.

"Come on."

"It's scary up there."

"I know," he says and grunts which means, Will you do it anyway? And then he keeps his chin tucked and rolls his eyeballs up to me, showing the white undersides, looking more like a slow reptile, a turtle whose shell has been crushed by teenage hooligans. It always works.

I take the attic stairs slowly, lifting both feet to each stair before advancing to the next in order to give any scary thing living in our attic fair warning that I'm coming and that it should clear out. There is a row of hanging garment bags and behind them a dark area in the eaves that is blocked by the bags. Anyone or anything could live up here.

Along the shore when I was young my mother, father, and I used to comb through the debris that storms would deposit on the beach. The sand and seaweed coated everything and made each log and shell and forgotten beach towel look the same. The sand hid the valuable things— baseball caps, old photos, canvas bags of money—in with the driftwood. It required a slow and discerning eye to separate the worthwhile from the junk. My father had such an eye. "There's a work glove," he said once to me, and eyeballed it up ahead. I ran to grab it and clutched it quite close for a minute, until I realized that the strange weight inside the glove was not sand that had accumulated there but was rather the part of the glove's original owner that belonged inside the glove. The hand. I screamed and ran back to my parents. "It's not a glove. It's a hand. A HAND!" My mother and I turned back to run in the opposite direction, away from the hand, screaming. But my father had to see it for himself. That's the sort of person he is. He walked slowly to where I'd dropped the hand on the beach and he grabbed it as though he were shaking it, saying, "Pleased to meet you." He felt around on the fingers and decided to carry the hand back to where we were standing, me cowering behind my mother. When he got close enough so that we could see what he was carrying my mother and I turned and ran again, back to the car. That was where we were when he caught up with us. I saw the hand in his hand and I locked all of our car doors, locking him out. He knocked on my mother's window. She opened the window but only a crack. "What are you doing?" she asked.

"He's got a wedding ring on," my father said. "I think we should take the hand to the police." And then turning to me he said, "He might have kids."

"Put the hand in the trunk," my mother said through the window and she reached across the driver's seat to pop the trunk open. I leaned forward as far as I could away from the trunk. I thought that hand was the hand of death and I didn't want it to creep through the ventilation system and grab me.

The light in our attic has properties similar to those of the sand after a storm. The gray light coats and obscures things; for example, hands of death or drawers of type, in the gray darkness. The attic is long and narrow, filled with junk from floor to ceiling. When I reach the top of the stairs looking for the fonts, there is a moment when my eyes have to adjust to the attic's darkness. That moment paralyzes me. The moment opens wide like a door. I see a man standing in the gray against the back wall of the house. The man looks at me and then cocks his head slowly to the left. He stares like water in a way that lets me know that if I don't do my job as a mermaid, somebody else will, a bounty hunter from the ocean. He lets me know that the water is coming for Jude or maybe it is coming for me. I know this man. I stop breathing. I try to make a sound for help but with no air there is no sound. Despite being frozen in place, my eyes adjust to the dark and as they do the man dissolves into a lamp with a guitar propped up behind it. I make a mad dash for the drawer of Palatino and the closer I get to the drawer, to the back of the attic where the man had disappeared, I notice something that I wish I hadn't. I grab the drawer and look once very quickly. I shouldn't have looked. There are footprints on the attic floor and they are wet. There are wet footprints where I saw the man. I run.

THE Cs

I think I will never make it back to the stairs. I am running and so the letters are spilling out of the tray. A B D E F H H H H H H. Some letters spill under my feet while I run. An H is my two legs, my two arms, and the bridge between. A whole compartment of Cs bumps from the tray and they roll under my feet. At the top of the stairs I trip on the letters. I Z, Y, N. I C on my back at the bottom of the stairwell. I hit my head, slamming it straight into unconsciousness.

When I wake up at the bottom of the stairs my mother and grandfather are there petting my head, saying, "Honey, honey, wake up, honey." I try to move. The drawer of type has spilled below me, cutting letters into my skin. The attic stairs creak and the spilled letters cut me.

"Oh," I say. "Ouch." They help me up. My grandfather is old and not too strong, but he gets me into my bed. "You guys, someone was up there, something wet," I tell them.

"Probably the rain," my mother says.

"No," I say. "Go look for yourself." But they don't. They are scared. My head hurts so badly that I want to close my eyes. My grandfather pets my head so I do close my eyes. I fall asleep and even though my mother wakes me up once an hour making sure that I don't have a concussion, I sleep through until the following morning.

The bruises that form one day later are in the shape of the letters I fell on. By afternoon they grow into one big black and blue, like an entire essay. These bruises are so odd that I think I will use them to write a note for Jude that says *m'aidez*, Mayday.

I drive over to Jude's house that afternoon once the boat he is working on has come in. I want to show him my letter bruises. I want Jude to touch the bruises as if they are Braille letters, as if he has to use his fingertips to read the words on my hips and back.

It doesn't work out that way exactly. He lets me in but I become too shy to mention the bruises when I see him.

The curtains of his living room are drawn closed, a sliver of sunlight sneaks in and illuminates all the particles floating in the air of Jude's house. I sit down in the light and so does Jude. He tells me a few stories about things like a type of fish caught in schools and used in the fabrication of ladies' makeup. He tells me about an idea he has for an opera where all the gods of all the religions of the world battle it out in song. He tells me about a fisherman he knows who loves the ocean so much that he had a tidal wave tattooed on his back. But Jude almost never tells me about the war, even if I ask, so I fear it won't ever go away, it won't ever get washed out to sea. Jude pours himself a glass of brown whiskey. Finally my shyness dissolves. "Look," I say, and lift just the back of my T-shirt.

"Fuck," he says. "What the hell happened?"

"I fell," I say.

And then he does touch me just as I had imagined, very lightly with his fingertips. He reads the weird words on my back. He stares and reads and finishes another drink. And when he is done reading he says, "That's scary." The words look dark and bruised.

"It's even scarier than you think," I say. "There was a man in the attic. That's why I fell."

"A man?" he asks. "What man?"

I do not answer. Jude is touching my back. Jude does not know that I am a mermaid.

He thinks the words are a warning, that something frightening or dangerous is lurking nearby. To him it is probably the U.S. Government wanting him to reenlist. To me, I don't tell him, it is my father.

"Let's get out of here," he says, and stands looking down at me. "This town," he says, "Let's go." He walks away to find the keys to his truck. "Really," he yells from the kitchen. The truck's engine turns over and I run outside. Finally, I think. I don't even bother to close the door to his house.

I am happy to leave town, to take a drive. I feel weightless and free, even if we don't go too far. But ten miles outside of town on the road an eighteen-wheeler carrying liquid oxygen has jackknifed, then toppled, then cracked open on the road in front of us. As the liquid hits the warmer air it evaporates in a cloud of thick steam. The idea of liquid oxygen makes me so thirsty, as though water or even the bottle of whiskey Jude brought along for the drive will never do after having sampled liquid air. The spill is evaporating and a police officer waves Jude's truck into the steam of it. There is a dip in the temperature. I roll down the window because the police officer is a boy I know from grade school. I ask him, "Is love like oxygen?" It is a song I thought he would have remembered. I thought he would have remembered me too, but he doesn't seem to understand and asks me, "Are you with the union?" he speaks above my head, addressing the question to Jude.

"No."

"Well then I suggest you and your vehicle turn around and head back to town. We have got a highly flammable situation here."

Jude says to me, "I see how it is. We *can't* leave town."

"This highway is going to be closed for hours. I suggest you head back to town," the policeman says very slowly.

Once I was pulled over by another police officer. The only thing I could think to tell him after he gave me a ticket was that he must have been born in the Sucksville County Hospital. The problem I have with authority isn't because I'm particularly wild, but the idea of supervision. I know the way I see the world is more super than a policeman who charges me $55 for a U-turn in a dead intersection. If they asked him what he saw he'd say, "a car, a light, a solid line." That's not super vision. But ask me what I saw. From here he looks like, Head. Brick. Head brick. Headbrick headbrickheadbrick.

"You hear me?" the policeman says. "Back to town." Jude doesn't answer but turns his truck around. We head back to town, defeated, silent, scared.

NO NAME

Even though Jude is much older than I am he still seems just right. I try to convince him of the fit by saying, "See that old man? He eats dinner alone at Friendly's almost every night," or, "You're an Aquarius too? All this time. You're an Aquarius too? Jude, I'm Aquarius. I never knew," or when he traces a path of blue blood just below the skin on my face I say, "I have got more just like that one. I'm nineteen," I tell him and I mean I'm old enough. "I'm nineteen," I tell him, and he groans.

There is a woman in town who once was so in love with Donny Osmond that she became a Mormon to be like him. Now that she is in her thirties she is still a Mormon, and Donny Osmond hasn't cut a popular album in years.

This woman's story makes me feel rot in all things I touch. I try to distract myself from thinking of Jude because I don't want to end up like her. I read books or instruction manuals or cereal boxes all day. I take baths to wash him off me, but then eventually I do end up thinking of him and I'll try to finger that Beatles song on my mother's piano so that I can sing his name underneath my breath while I bite the inside of my cheek hard enough to make it taste like metal type that would spell his name.

I spend most of my time here waiting. Waiting to grow up. Waiting for my father to return. Waiting for Jude. Waiting for something big to happen. I wait in the water of my bathtub. I lie curled on one side under the water. In elementary school a teacher told me our bodies are ninety-five percent water. I don't see how this could be true. Still, I'm keen to believe him. Under the water I open my eyes. Because of the ocean we don't have wells. All the groundwater here is salty. We have town water that they add chlorine to so no one gets sick. The chlorine burns my eyes and some days my bath smells like a swimming pool.

In the bath, once the water is in my ears, ninety-five percent water becomes ninety-six percent. I swallow a gulp of bathwater, ninety-eight percent. That is as close as I get. I sit up with my knees bent and wait for the water to still. The water breaks my shins. I do have shins. I do have legs. To be one hundred percent water I would have to get my entire body under the surface and then some. I am small but I am going to need more water.

I move in the tub and the water begins to lap from side to side making a ruckus. Just then I hear a floorboard creak outside the bathroom door and my heart jumps up into my mouth. It tastes like a bad word. I stand bolt upright in the bathwater, prepared to defend myself. I think of the gray man from the attic. I think of a bunch of bounty hunters as a swarm of black flies just outside the door. I strain to hear what is moving in the hallway but I have disturbed the water by standing. It is making a splashing noise, giving away my location to whatever spooky thing is creeping around outside the bathroom door. A floorboard creaks again, long and low, as if in pain. I breathe heavily. My blood rushes away from my lungs and flows instead to my ears that are trying so hard to hear the bad thing in the hallway that has come to get me.

"Hey," the bad thing says outside the door. I suck in my breath. "Hi. It's Jude."

I don't answer him. He might walk in and I am standing naked in two feet of water. Plus I left some pee unflushed in the toilet. He opens the door but does not step inside yet. I cover my stomach with my hands and arms. I cover where I am the bluest. I hear him breathe and in he walks. He stands a bit frozen and stares like a bridge between his eyes and my body. Eventually the bathwater calms down. I tuck my chin to my chest. "What are you looking at?" I ask him. Jude sees but doesn't answer. "Get out," I say but he doesn't move. I shut my eyes. I feel like my skin has never seen the light of day. Jude imagines that without moving. Like he's the first. I lift my head. I don't want to be the Mormon girl in love with Donny Osmond. I listen to him breathe and I stare at the oldness of his hands. He watches me until the air between us feels as thick as electricity right at the transformer.

He starts to tell me a story while he stares at me. He has a seat without looking away. "There was a town north of the Kuwaiti border. It was tiny. We only knew it by number coordinates, not by name," Jude says. He rubs his hands across his thighs. I imagine I am between them. "They didn't tell us the name on purpose because bad things had happened there, things that broke the rules of war. Its coordinates were on a list, an Army list of words we were never supposed to say, so that if we ever encountered someone from the media and we didn't know they were with the media we wouldn't slip and mention, 'fear,' or, 'intestines,' or, 'bodies hung out to dry like laundry on a clothesline,' or the name of that town, or any other phrase that was on the official list of things we weren't supposed to say." Jude looks at me. "My palms are getting wet," he says and looks down at them. "I feel like your name was on that list. Like you are off limits. Like if I say your name or if I touch you, I'd get court-martialed, found guilty, and executed."

I don't say anything.

He stares and stares. "Sorry," he says and starts to back out the door. "I thought there was something wrong with you," he says. "Your mother told me you had been in the water forever."

I stand naked, looking at Jude, concentrating on becoming one hundred percent water so that I could slip down the drain and out to sea or at least I could slip down Jude's wrong pipe and fill his lungs, lovingly washing away every breath he takes.

THE KNIGHT

I feel a bit funny after Jude has left, like I forgot to trick him in some way that I was supposed to know but had forgotten or had never learned because I'm not from here. Instead I felt like *I* had been tricked. Again. And an old defense from grade school welled up in me. I went up to our roof. I hadn't been there in awhile. Not since the day four boys in my tenth grade class covered the hair on my head with duct tape. They told me it was a scientific experiment so I let them do it.

When I was young I retreated here rather often because from the peak of the roof I would will myself to imagine the entire town getting flooded and filled as the ice caps melted, as the ocean crept higher and higher. From my roof I thought I'd watch those boys sputter and drown. It wasn't an experiment. I thought if they tried to grab hold of my roof while the water was rising, I would walk over to the rain-gutter edge and squish their pale fingers underneath my tennis shoe, though usually in my imagining I had on my father's steel-toed work boots because they were more effective at finger crushing.

The dormer window out to the roof is already open. I swing one leg through and the rest of my body follows. My mother is already sitting on the roof. "Mama," I say very quietly at first, scared to startle her when we're up so high.

"Hi," she says, while I scramble up the incline to where she is seated. A few old houses in town have widow's walks—the small square rooms or flat platforms built into a roof so that women left behind by fishermen husbands could look out to see if their men's ships were ever going to come in. We don't have a widow's walk, so my mother sometimes just sits on the roof with binoculars around her neck. She acts as if she's just looking at the ocean, the birds, or the waves but I know she is looking for my father. From here we can see just about everything, all the houses in town and past them the ocean straight out to the horizon line.

"What are you doing?" I ask.

"Just reading." She shows me the book. "It's about a mermaid. I have been looking for it. I wanted to give it to you. But your grandfather had it filed in the **G**s, for 'German author,' he said."

"What happens?" I ask.

"It's not good," she says. "Her name is Undine. Your grandfather says the word is Teutonic and means a female from the water. Undines like humans. They are soulless unless they marry a mortal."

I smile a bit, as if saying I told you so.

"Why are you smiling?" She turns to me. "Why would you want to be soulless? It's a sad story. This Undine." She holds up the book. "She falls in love with a knight named Huldbrand and Huldbrand loves Undine too, but he also loves her stepsister, Bertalda, a mortal. So Undine's uncle, he's a river spirit, is disgraced. He takes Undine back down under the water and tells her she must kill Huldbrand or else he will."

"What does she do?" I ask.

My mother looks at me and pulls her shoulders back, pulling away from me to gauge my reaction. "Undine kills him."

"Oh." I look away while she stares. She is making me nervous and so the very tips of my lips curve microscopically into a smile. But because she is my mother, she sees it, the microscopic smile. "Why would you want to be anything like that?" she asks. "You're nineteen. Why would you want to hitch yourself to some sinking ship like Jude? I mean Jude's nice, but you're young. You should travel. You should move to New York City. See the world. Meet people." She turns away to look out towards the ocean.

I don't really like people, I think. That's why.

Just then her expression grows wide and she raises her binoculars to her eyes. "What's that?" She stands up, excited and pointing to a spot where the waves break. There is something floating there, some sort of mass—trash or a rain slicker or maybe just a seal. I suppose it could look like a man, but not if you looked at it for too long.

"It's a log, Mom. Or a trash bag."

"Are you sure?"

I nod yes. "Yeah, Mom."

"Because for a second," she says, and breaks the thought off there.

"For a second you thought it was Dad?"

She looks at me with a twisted mouth. Her mouth is twisted from having told me to do one thing while she always does the exact opposite.

"You should move to New York City," I tell her, and she nods slowly and very slightly without looking away from whatever it is floating in the sea foam.

Jude has a headache. I tell him to lie down. I tell him I'll rub his head. We are at his house. I rub the crown of his head and his temples. I am nervous. I fear I am doing a bad job, that he won't like it, but after a few moments I feel him relax his neck and jaw and I am glad.

Sitting this way, his neck is very close to me and his blood is only millimeters away from that. Having Jude's blood this close makes me think of wrought iron in taste and texture, like the bumpy veins of a man or a horse, and it's so rare that anything on land will make a warm bit of difference to me, sunk as I am. I'd take Jude's neck down under the water and for few minutes it would still be red and hot as a horseshoe in heat.

He closes his eyes and I'd like to wrap my arms around him. I'd like to push the hair from his face and trace the lines of his nose. I'd like to hold my finger below his nostrils for a long time, until it is damp from his exhalations. Then I'd put the finger in my mouth and drink Jude's breath. It probably would taste like alcohol but I forgive him for that. There is little else to do here besides get drunk and it seems to make what is small, us, part of something that is drowned and large, something like the bottom of the sea, something like outer space. Drinking helps us continue living in remote places because, thankfully, here there is no one to tell us just how swallowed we are.

"I like you," Jude says. He opens his eyes. He has small drops of sweat bulbing on his brow.

"I like you," I say, and more than anything I do. Jude would never make me think of a timetable or a bank account or a good job, whatever the fuck that means. He'd never make me think of any of the ugly things on dry land. Despite all that is not right with Jude, nothing I do with him is ever held up to the light for judgment. He never thinks I am odd or weird or poor or perverted or wrong. He'd never say, "You're a real nut job." I'd sit in his dirty laundry for days and he would understand. He would even bring me a cup of soup while I sat.

I want to tell Jude what it was like when he went to the war, what it was like to be waiting at home for him and wondering whether or not he would be killed. But I never do. I don't want it to be a competition about which of us suffered more. I never tell him that when he was in the war I tried to wrap my arms around the dresser in my bedroom. My cheek was doughy from sleeping where I'd been crying and the dresser's corner left a red imprint. "Kiss me," I said and kicked its leg when it didn't. The varnish smelled sticky and old, like Worcestershire sauce. I stuck out my tongue to taste it but became scared that the emptiness of the dresser would suck me into its vacuum. I let go.

Or that when Jude was in the war I opened up the hole in my chest. I stored some new things there. There was plenty of room. Things like nail clippers, thread, addresses. Those things easy to lose that drive you mad to find. But every time I went to find them, they'd be gone.

When Jude was in the war I liked to imagine how difficult it was to get my letters past the war censors with their big black markers. I doubt that there are actually censors anymore, but I'd imagine them all the same. Sometimes I thought that what I had written to him would arrive looking like this:

Dear Jude,
Today my ▓▓▓ *and I found a* ▓▓ *It was*
a ▓▓ *with black and* ▓▓ *spots on its*
▓▓ *.*
Love,

▓▓▓▓▓

When Jude was in the war I cleaned empty hotel rooms for money. In most of the rooms a man had taken a woman or girl and loved her with her face against the wall so she couldn't see him. When I cleaned at the motel I'd touch the wall with my own face. I'd pretend he was behind me. I couldn't see him. He was in the war. The walls tasted like salt. Imagine how the wall and the women and the girls feel through each winter and each war, standing with their faces up against a wall, playing one love scene they recall over and over again, like a video movie or the memory of something that broke.

TEST CASE

I know this is not uncommon, but I've always required very little prompting to convince myself that this is a scientific experiment. Just my life, specifically. Almost everyone else is in on it. Jude's either innocent or he's the lead scientist. I've always wanted to be a scientist so I've tried to make friends on the other side, people who might risk passing me a dangerous hint from the resistance, saying, "There are others like you." That hasn't happened yet.

Jude gets paid daily when he fishes and if he's done well he'll come by the house. "Let me take you out to lunch," he says, because he has a small pile of money. We usually go out for Chinese food. Jude's hair looks Chinese, soft and black like a Chinese crow. I wonder how the two pieces of evidence work together in the experiment.

"Jude, have you ever thought that your life was an experiment?" I ask.

"Why yes," he says. "Yes I have," he coughs. "I think that's an entirely natural thought."

I see. He's trying to throw me off the scent. I knew it.

"Testing," Jude says. "Testing," because he pays for our lunch and he stares at me silently for extended periods of time. On my side of the experiment those actions commonly mean, "Take me home with you and kiss me." But Jude drives me to my house. "See you tomorrow," he says and leaves. Sometimes he'll even go before I can get my keys out of my pocketbook. I tell myself, "He's got to get over to the lab and type up a report: Subject delusional— she wholly believes in the elements we fabricated for this experiment, namely,

love

death

ocean

mercy

The words fall like drops in some ancient water torture. When I get home I tell my mother, "I've always wanted to be a scientist." I am hoping that if I tell her this again she will let me in on the experiment.

She doesn't. Instead she says, "I've always wanted to be a Christian Scientist. Why don't we become Christian Scientists together?" She is not serious. She knows little of that church—the same bit most of us know about their not going to doctors. She thinks that she would like to be one of them because of how, years ago, she lost a baby at the hospital. She wishes she had become a Christian Scientist before she went to the hospital. I tell her, "The baby was dead inside you before you got there." But she likes to blame the hospital.

"What does their name mean?" I ask her. "Why are they scientists?"

I am thinking that if she says, "Because they conduct secret experiments instead of going to church," I will join up. But she doesn't answer me. She stands staring out the window, holding the hole in her belly.

METAMORPHOSIS

It is early. I can't rest. So I walk to Jude's house while the street is still asleep. The street is dreaming it is the silver asphalt of fish scales, and it looks that way, too. Jude's house is locked up. I go around back and lie down on the small stair landing outside, though it is cloudy. I imagine the curves of the woman he has in there and his hands on them. While I wait I hear lots of things, particularly one noise that sounds like choking and I think, "Good. He has killed her." I sit up.

Beside me on the staircase is the molted exoskeleton of an insect and the insect who has come from inside. The exoskeleton looks like a brown paper bag, though the insect's old hands and feet and antennae are exact, not like a bag but like the real thing. The insect, now outside its spent skin, looks damp and buttery. It becomes apparent that eventually, in a few minutes, the insect will unfold itself into a dragonfly. I can tell by the silica wings, still sticky.

Eventually Jude opens the door but only he comes out. I look inside behind him. "I didn't know you were here," he says.

No one else is with him. In the short time that I waited for Jude, not too long, the dragonfly matured enough to fly away. So I hated it because I knew that would never happen to me.

MUTINY, BOUNTY

We've been fogged in for five days. The fog makes me both love and hate the weather. I hate it because it brings me down, but I love it because if the foul state continues I won't have to do anything important with my life, and in many ways I am quite happy in that knowledge.

The television talks about those who couldn't make it through the winter. People who ran out of oil over a weekend or had a slippery car wreck, or a man who went overboard in the weight of a net, or someone who got electrocuted listening to the storm radio in the bathtub, or someone whose liver finally gave out from drinking too much.

Karen, the deaf girl, was here for dinner and though she's gone now my mother is still feeling quiet. She is sitting in the doorway between the kitchen and the living room reading a book about the Italian Mafia. Jude and I are trying to watch television for the fourth night in a row but my grandfather interrupts. He has been reading some odd dictionaries I got him at the library's yearly sell-off. One is a Russian-to-English from the 1950s. "I don't think you'll believe what I found," he says. "A word, can't pronounce it. We don't have a word to match it but we should. We should develop it tonight because the word means, 'the feelings one retains for someone he once loved.'"

"Hate?" Jude says.

"No, not that feeling." My grandfather looks at Jude with disappointment.

"Betrayal," my mother says without looking away from her book.

"No. It's the little house love moved out of, maybe a hermit crab moves in and carries the house across the floor of a tidal pool. The lover sees the old love moving and it looks like it's alive again."

They are all wrong. There's a reason why we have no word for it. You don't get to keep the feelings for someone you once loved. Once you've washed your hands of that person, all those feelings, all that dirty water is washed out to sea. There is no word for that dirty water.

The three of them argue. They try to develop an English word to match.

"How about 'disamoured?'" my grandfather proposes.

"Or 'screart,'" Jude suggests.

"What about 'evol?'" my mother says, and smiles. They look at me for an idea too. I don't say anything. "Once loved" is not my specialty as I haven't stopped yet. I step out our back door.

The night is cold and beautiful. Though there is still a layer of damp moisture close to the earth, higher up the fog has lifted some and I can see a few stars for the first time in days. I crane my neck, looking overhead, studying the constellations for a long while. I used to know some of their names but have not studied the sky for so long that I have trouble remembering. I would be better off if I developed my own system of constellations, and that way I wouldn't forget what Ursus or Pleiades or Orion is supposed to look like. I could make letters from the stars and have them spell words that I'd never forget. That way I would know the sky. I would be able to navigate accordingly. Looking up I start to spell. J, I see. I spell. U. I look around the sky. D, I see, and scroll across the stars looking for the next letter. I cannot find an E. My neck is getting rigid, my head filled with blood. That is how I know, how I can feel a tingling. Someone is watching me.

I right my head. The rest of my body freezes. I scan the yard, moving just my eyeballs, until I think I see him. My breath is labored with fear so that it is all I can hear. "What do you want?" I ask, and just then my eyes focus for a moment against the wood of the shed that has grayed in the weather. I see him. He is shaking his head no, no, no. Only this time I recognize him. "Dad." I try not to blink. I stare and am certain it's him. "Daddy," I say, because I haven't seen him since I was eight years old. He is wearing a very old denim shirt. It is torn and sodden. It is the same shirt. He is wearing his rubber boots. The same rubber boots. "Daddy." My eyes are getting dry but I'm scared he'll disappear if I blink. My eyes start to tear. He dissolves.

I walk very carefully, very slowly over to the shed. I am scared even though I know it was him. I am scared that something will jump out at me. I touch the wood where he stood. He came from the water and the wall is wet. Without turning I back away and shake my head just like he did in case he is still watching. Because I understand what he is saying to me. I run for our door. I lock it and pull the curtain shut, like a blanket over Jude.

EROSION

Scientists have found that the significant asteroid named Eros demonstrates signs of erosion. I am not making this up. The scientists have trouble figuring out why this is happening since there is no wind and no water in outer space to make erosion happen. I am nineteen and Jude is thirty-three. I think the only way I'll catch up to him here, where we have water and wind, is for him to stop growing. He is outside my house and sees me in the window. He waves hello. Or for me to get old quickly, and so I wonder what the force is that is eroding the asteroid named Eros and wonder where I can get myself some before my father comes back again.

"I'm tree. I'm tree," the little boy who lives next door says to Jude, and holds up his pinky, ring, and middle fingers to demonstrate. Last week that boy asked me, "Do you love ice cream?" and I told him that, yes, I did. So he asked me, "Then why don't you marry it?" and ran behind my house laughing.

Jude says to the boy, "Why, buddy, I think it's three." It sounds like, "My bonnie lies under the sea." I haven't come out of my room yet since last night. I am too scared. I haven't told any of them, not even my mother. I am too scared. They won't believe me. I hear Jude come inside the house. He is downstairs with my grandfather. If Jude comes to my door I will ask him before I let him in, "Jude, do you love me?" and I think he'll say yes, so I'll ask him, "Then why don't you marry me?" Because I have never heard of even one mermaid story where the mermaid's family does not come up out of the sea to kill the mortal man who won't marry the mermaid. They always come to get their daughters back.

The scientists working on asteroids suspect that the erosion on Eros is caused by magnetic fields and magnetic storms. The friction in attraction. I am certain that I will erode faster than Jude.

I learned about the asteroid Eros while I was visiting our local library with my mother. Oddly enough there were people receiving flu shots in the library among the books, of all the places. There were bright red bags to dispose of the used needles. The bags were clearly marked BIOMEDICAL HAZARD among all those books. There

are many things to make me angry here, many unbeauti-
ful things, but I know the ice caps really are melting and
it fortifies me when I remember that all these ugly park-
ing places, all these red bags, will be on the bottom of the
ocean soon. At the library I saw a photo in the newspaper of dark and open water near the North Pole. When
the ice caps melt, volumetrically speaking, there becomes
more of it, so it is a concern for people who live on islands or people who have homes too close to the water.
In the North where I live, the land is still bounding back
up from the weight of the ice that once covered it. Each
year the ground moves skyward in fractions. However, it
is not moving fast enough. It would be best to get used
to the water. I will try to tell people in town. I will go
with Jude to the bars and strike up conversations with
other drinkers. "It's coming," I will say. I will tell them
about the biologists who found that whales evolved from
something cow-like, something rhinoceros-like. "Whales
evolved into the water!" I will say. It is possible, and not a
backwards evolution. I will urge the bar patrons to prac-
tice in their bathtubs. I will repeat, "It's coming." They
will think I mean Jesus and the horsemen. But I don't. So
I will tell them, "Well, the horsemen should remember
how to swim."

Jude is out back helping my mother move some
flagstones. I can see his arm muscle peeking out of his
T-shirt. I notice my mother is also looking at Jude's round

arm muscle and for a moment I am angry at her. I look up at the ceiling in my bedroom and think that there must be a leak here in the house where the wind and weather has gotten to me. The leak follows me from room to room and drips on my head even when there is no rain. It is eroding me. It used to follow my father, but since he's gone it follows me. This dripping torture waters down how I see things. This drip fills the tub upstairs. From the tub I tell my father, "I know you are very mad that Jude doesn't love me. You are right to be mad. He has misled me," but as soon as I say it I want the words back. I drag my fingers through the bathwater. One "very" left. No sign of "Jude" or "misled" or "you are right." Just like water to take the best words quickly.

SINKING

The following day I finally come downstairs. My mother is in the kitchen. She is making a cup of tea and the two of us watch the odd direction steam takes in exiting her teacup. "Are you sure you don't want any?" she asks.

"Umhm."

There's no draft or movement in the room but the steam is making it very clear that there are certain strata in the kitchen's invisible air that are denser than others, and so the steam avoids them and wraps itself between them like rope.

"Are you feeling better?" she asks. I nod my head yes. "I couldn't sleep last night," she says. "I went out with Jude after we finished up here," she says. "He wanted to get drunk."

"What'd he say?"

"Well, he asked if I would have a drink with him."

"Oh." I say. "Did you?"

"I did. Yes. I'm sorry. I did."

"I don't give a fuck," I say, and stand to leave, but the word "fuck" has lowered a ceiling, making these certain strata in the kitchen's invisible air even denser than before. I swat the air, trying to get it behind me but instead I end up spilling my mother's tea into her lap. Which makes her scream. I didn't mean to do it.

"I'm sorry, Momma."

"It was an accident," she says and goes upstairs to lie down and put a cool towel on the burn. She is in her bed and I bring her some ointment. I bring her a cup of tea.

"Don't be scared of me, please," I say to her.

"Shh," she says. "It was an accident," she says and takes the cup of tea from me. "Sit here," she says and pats the corner of her bed, right up close to her. I sit down. "What's making you so sad?" she asks me.

I lift my shoulders up to my ears to say, "I don't know" or, "Don't ask me" without actually having to say either.

"Did something happen with Jude?" she asks.

"No," I say. "That is the problem. Nothing ever happens with Jude."

"I see," she says. "Well nothing happened between me and Jude either, if that's what you thought. If that's why you spilled tea on me."

"It was an accident."

"I know. I know," she says.

Then I tell her, "Last night I was in the bath and I tried to speak to Dad. I told him, 'Jude is a stone.'"

"Your father's dead," she says and bites her lip. Then asks, "What'd he say?"

"He said, 'If Jude is a stone then he should sink like one.' So I let the water out of the tub." I turn toward her. "I don't want to be the mermaid who kills Jude, Mom."

"Oh," she says in a voice that sounds like the voice of a mother whose daughter just broke something, a piece of china or crystal and she is trying not to get mad about it. But in this instance, though, the thing that my mother believes is broken is me.

SCIENTOLOGY EXPERIMENT

The Church of Scientology sent us a personality test in the mail. They send them to us on a monthly basis because they want us to join them. Many of the words within the quiz are inappropriately enclosed in quotation marks. For example, Do you keep "close contact" on articles of yours that you have loaned to friends? Could you agree to "strict discipline?" Are you "always getting into trouble?" Are you always collecting things that "might be useful?" Do you "wax enthusiastic" about only a few subjects? Do you ever get disturbed by the noise of the wind or a "house settling down?" Would it take a "definite effort" on your part to consider the subject of suicide? Do you browse through "dictionaries" just for pleasure? These are the real questions. I didn't make them up.

I am reviewing my answers at our kitchen table. I have the front windows open so that a breeze blows the questionnaire off the table and down to the floor in front of the refrigerator. The paper stays at the bottom of the refrigerator and I remain still. I am beginning to deduce that Scientology is not the same as science at all. The questionnaire scoots across the linoleum in the breeze. It blows beneath the table and I crumple my test underfoot.

Jude is in love with something watery.

My father told me I am a mermaid.

Therefore Jude must be in love with me.

But the above logic is faulty. Lots of things besides me are watery. Alcohol is watery. Water is watery.

I devise my own test. I fill the tub on the third floor. I get in and put my head under the water, blowing bubbles. The test asks, Do you "miss your father" when it rains? Do you stay in this "God-forsaken town" because you think he is still here? Do you only like men who could match your father "drink for drink?" Don't you know "drinkers" only love drinking? Can you "breathe" underwater? Are you really a mermaid or does it just feel that way in the awkward body of a "teenage girl?" I breathe water into my lungs. I wait for my test results.

UNDER

When I surface Jude is there. "Jude," I say, but there is something covering my mouth, a nozzle with oxygen. Jude cannot breathe under the water. I pass him the nozzle of oxygen that is attached to my nose. He refuses and wraps it again behind my ears. We are not underwater. We are in an ambulance. An EMT is taking my heart rate. I can hear her as she yells, "Sinking! Sinking!" The back doors open and four people carry me into the hospital on this bed. I can't see much except for the fluorescent lights passing overhead. I'm brought to a small room for more yelling. "Evacuate those lungs! Pump!" one doctor yells. Then I feel a needle enter the vein of my elbow and I don't remember falling asleep.

When I wake all three of them—Jude, my mother, and my grandfather—are there. There is also a doctor. At first it is difficult to open my eyes. The doctor sees I am waking up from the drug. The doctor says, "Young lady, what you've done is quite serious." I try to look at him. I can't quite keep my eyes open. I hear what the doctor is saying to my mother. "I don't understand why she is still alive. Her lungs were sodden, filled with water. She should be dead," he says and then, "It's a miracle." My mother asks the doctor to leave. My mother wants to issue all the scolding I deserve herself.

I am beginning to see what putting my head under the bathwater looks like to them.

My grandfather is holding my chart. He is nervous. "Franklin Gothic," he says identifying the font they used to print my chart.

My mother looks at me. "Gothic. Right."

"Momma." I clear my throat. "I wasn't trying to die." But she turns away, crying.

The drug is making me feel ill. I'd like to leave this place. I look at my arms and legs under the covers. I am unattached. I try to sit up. I want to leave but my mother stops me. "No," she says. "You have to stay here."

When I was young I went down to the pier looking for my father. I accidentally got on board the wrong boat. The boat was out at sea before the sailors found me. I gave them a big surprise. Three thousand different aquatic life forms are carried daily into new ecosystems by unsuspecting ship's ballast.

I was scared on board, surrounded by five sailors. I thought that the captain was a pirate because he had a round bite taken out of his ear. To appease him I told him I'd work to pay for my passage. "What can you do?" he asked, and for a long time I had to think. I told him I knew how to set type. He shook his head. "I don't need a typesetter. I've got a brand new dot-matrix printer." Eventually I told him I would make a good end table or hassock. "Great," he said. So I curled up on the dirty floor and prepared for work. I waited for some weight on my back but it never came.

After awhile the captain said, "Come on now. Get up, sweetheart." Which scared me. If there wasn't going to be a legitimate trade he was probably going to steal something from me. But he didn't. Instead, he gave me ice cream and told me I was a brave girl. Still, after the ice cream, I continued working and soon I was a hassock asleep.

My mother always tells this story whenever she meets someone new. She thinks it is funny. It embarrasses me because the person my mother tells, for a moment, thinks of me as sea captain's furniture, which, I believe, most people consider out of date or made from oddly colored Naugahyde. Though it is a truthful representation of me—oddly colored, out of date—I still am embarrassed.

The three thousand foreign forms of aquatic life introduced daily into unfamiliar ecosystems usually don't survive but, more commonly, float to the surface and get burned by the sun.

When I was returned to my family I continued to work as a hassock around our house, and sometimes my father would actually use me, resting his feet while he watched the television. I liked the job because it reminded me of the sailors I had met on board.

In this hospital I am embarrassed. Jude looks peculiar here. His paleness is awkward against the maize-colored walls. My mother and grandfather are both too pink and healthy to be here. I'm embarrassed because I want to look foreign here, as they do, and float to the top, get burned by the sun. I want to not belong here. I'm a mermaid. How can I belong in a hospital on dry land? But the gown I have on matches the sheets and there is a label around my wrist saying, "This is where you belong." So I tuck my head and curl into a ball waiting for weight—something hard or sharp from Jude, a fist or a scream. It never comes. He sits quietly, uncertain of what to say.

"I'm thirsty," I finally tell him.

Jude has not said anything. He pours me a glass of water, but while carrying it to the bed it falls from his hand. The water explodes out of the plastic cup and Jude immediately slips on the water. His head nearly smashes my mechanical bed.

"Shit!" my mother screams because she is completely on edge.

"Hahaha," the water says and it sounds like my father.

"Did you hear that?" I ask. But they ignore me. "Jude, the water is coming to get you," I say, and then the three of them exchange glances of the saddest kind. My mother looks down at my hands as if to look in my eyes would make her start crying again. She looks at my hands as though I am strange to her.

"Jude, are you all right?" she asks. She bends to help him.

"I'm fine. I'm fine," he says and has a seat in a hospital chair. We sit for awhile in silence.

Eventually I do get more visitors. The men in blue. The men in white. And my grandmother, Marcella. She is somewhere in between them like a beautiful horizon line. My grandmother Marcella doesn't say much but holds up her finger to make a division.

Wet. Dry.

Sea. Sky.

Dead. Alive.

I have to stay at the hospital for three days. I'm required to undergo evaluation. That "undergo" is the word I keep using, as it somehow suggests a passage or secret tunnel to the doctor's office. There is no secret tunnel though.

In his office the doctor looks at my chart. "Huh. Had some eye trouble, I see," he says.

"I don't. Not very well."

"Now this eye trouble, it says here, there's nothing physically wrong with your eyes. How does that make you feel?"

"I'm thirsty."

"I see."

"I don't. Not very well."

"Let's talk about what happened in the bathtub." The doctor says, "I've read the report—"

"Not read. Just blue."

"—patient tried to drown herself in the bath. How does that make you feel?"

"Give the chart to my grandfather. When it's returned it will read, in a nice Garamond or Bodoni, '—patience tried.' Because doctor, this making a mortal love me is tasking business and I'm running out of time. So I tried to drown myself. I want to go back to the ocean. That way I thought Jude could continue living. But you all ruined it." That's what I tell the doctor and he looks surprised by my answer. "I'm from the ocean," I add to clarify my position. The doctor writes that down. He gets up to leave and watches me from the door, and I think he understands me because in a few days, when the hospital finds out that my mother lied about us having health insurance, with some pamphlets and some pills, I am sent home.

DANGEROSE

At home I am ashamed. They all think I was trying to kill myself. I walk around sheepishly. I try to be helpful and quiet.

While I was in the hospital our basement flooded with two feet of water. It happens all the time. Our sump pump is nearly as old as the house and tired. I go into the cellar carrying a tiny dinghy constructed of corrugated fiberglass. My father made it for me when I was a little girl, and despite being a rough and tiny craft, it is still seaworthy. I row over to the fuse box to turn off all the power in the house before the flood reaches the fuses. I am trying to be helpful. I float for a bit in the dark basement. Overhead I can see dusty cobwebs and ceiling joists. The boat rocks some, and I could almost fall asleep down here but I don't. I don't want to scare my mother again. I row back to the bottom of the staircase and climb up into the sunlight.

I try to talk to my neighbors concerning the flood, but I can see that I make them nervous now. It seems all the neighbors also think I tried to drown myself in the bathtub. Still I tell them, "Our basement is flooded. Do you think this is the end?" At first they think I mean because of the terrorists. So I say, "No. Do you think the ocean is coming for us? Well, not me, but you?"

They shake their heads as if to say, "Poor child," but all they really say is, "Huh. That's strange," or they say, "You went to high school. You figure it out."

So I call Jude. He is glad I am home from the hospital. "Listen," I tell him, and I put the telephone up to the cellar door so he can hear the shore lapping beneath our living room floorboards. "What does it mean?" I ask.

"I don't know," he says and then, "How are you doing? Really?" So I hang up.

I go upstairs to ask my mother. She has been crying. She says she doesn't know what to do with me. I don't ask her about the flooding.

I ask my grandfather but he is old. He sets down the plate of dictionary he's been typesetting.

"What?" He pretends he can't hear me.

"The water! In the basement!"

"What?"

"Forget it," I say.

"Look what I wrote this morning." He shoves a plate of type in front of me.

danger–n. A charming, young lady named
Dangerose once yielded to the
importunities of Damase, the Lord of
Asnieres; defying the curses of Thigh, 37th
Bishop of Mans, they lived in love
together. One day as the Lord was crossing
a stream, a violent storm arose, stricken by
lightening and overwhelmed by the
waters, the wicked Damase was half-
burned, half-drowned, and passed to
perdition. The distraught Dangerose
threw herself at the Bishop's feet in
penitence; she lived thereafter in strict
retirement. But her story spread far; and
whenever anything drew peril after it, the
French said, "Ceci sent la Dangerose."

"You just made that up."

"I did not."

"Then you copied it." My grandfather tucks his chin to pretend he is hurt, but when I look at his face he's not hurt. He is laughing because he did copy it. "It's stolen." I scold him.

"Not stolen. It flew to me." He laughs a little.

I have to explain myself to him. "Grandpa, I wasn't trying to kill myself. I just thought that if I went back into the water then Jude wouldn't have to die, then Jude could meet a nice girl from the dry land and marry her and he'd stop drinking."

My grandfather nods his head. He can hear when he wants to. "That's one way of seeing it," he says.

My grandfather and I only disagree based on misalignments or misunderstandings from his age to mine. For instance he might yell, "Damn broken caps!" And I would think he means his bulbous red nose's broken capillaries. So I would say, "Well you shouldn't have drunk so much your whole life." But then he would look at me puzzled. He would be holding a piece of type, a capital B and the bottom curve has broken off. "Into the hellbox with you," he would say to the B. To me, too.

My grandfather has told me he remembers a time before longitude and latitude. That would make him older than I believe physically possible, but he insists that he remembers the headline: *Tiny Lines Circle the Globe! More on page 24.*

These longitude lines can cause problems for map printers—spreading a round thing, like the globe, to flat distorts the truth of what's between the lines. Mercator projection makes up solid land that's not actually there. Molehill Greenland makes a mountain. That made-up land, made-up sea near Greenland, is not too far away from where I live.

Jude runs his hand through his hair, but this town is flat and the space between each line of text, each strand of Jude's black hair, stretches out so that what I read is more than one width of truth. He runs his hand through his hair and the Mercator projection makes my ground shake. His fingers and his hair stretch like the longitude lines in my head so that his molehill, "You're too young," makes my mountain, "Rope, knife, gun."

My grandfather takes down an old map from the Constantinople Press while my mother walks into the kitchen. He spreads the map out before me while she looks over my shoulder. He points to Greenland. "This is how a nineteen-year-old girl sees a man like Jude," he says. "The Mercator projection. It's making Jude look a lot larger than he actually is. The truth is, Jude's a drunk from a very small place who doesn't say much because there's nothing to say."

I shake my head no. "Look at my map," I say, but I don't have a map.

"What are you talking about?" my mother asks, and while I think of how I can explain to them just how much I love Jude, she says, "Just don't get stuck here because of him. Don't get stuck like I did." She tucks her chin and starts to cry again. When she does this I can see the back of her head. There's something there, something gross.

She has a clump of seaweed stuck in her hair. It has dried there, like marooned debris that waits and waits and waits in the rocks for an extremely high tide to come sweep it back out to the ocean. It waits and rots and stinks.

"I have to go, you guys."

"That's what I am trying to tell you." My mother bites at her lip and my grandfather rolls his map. "It's dangerous to stay here," she says and stands up, coming towards me. But I feel scared. I back myself up against the countertop and wrap my arms across my chest for protection. Fear creeps up my back, and it is a fear so loud I find it difficult to hear my thoughts. My mother opens her arms to hug me, but I am so scared that I don't uncross my arms. She hugs me and speaks right into my ear in a whisper, "The water—" she says and then, "This is a small town," she says and then interrupts herself again. "You should get out now."

I stand still sort of hugging my mother, wondering does she mean this instant, now, or soon, within the month or year? I stand still, thinking about that, and she stands still hugging me, petting my neck and ear. We are so still that I can hear the sound of waves in the basement again. I can hear waves breaking on our cellar stairs, lapping higher and higher, coming closer. In that instant the fear in my spine, the water in the cellar, unleashes a screaming word to my brain, an answer, one simple word, and it's "Now!" I kiss my mother. I kiss my grandfather and run.

WAR AMONG THE MAYFLIES

At first I think of running to the police station, but Jude once dated a woman who works there and I remember that the night she met me she said, "Ah, what a cute girl. Isn't it after your bedtime?" I don't know what to tell the police anyway. If I said, "I am a mermaid, but a good one. I don't want to kill anybody. But my father, that's another story," they might lock me up. I run to Jude's. If the water's coming to get him at least I can try to protect him.

He lets me in and for ten minutes we don't talk. I haven't seen him since I got home from the hospital. He just waits while I catch my breath. Finally he says, "Listen. You've got enough trouble without me." He is very serious about it. He pulls a bottle of Canadian whiskey down off the refrigerator. "We've got to stop seeing each other."

"Why?"

"Well something seems to be pulling you apart, and I don't want it to be me. Your mother, well, she thought you were acting a bit delusional."

"Oh, my mother called *me* delusional? Well, where does she think that came from?"

"She just wants something different for you."

Jude pours us both a small glass of whiskey, and as he places my glass on the kitchen table in front of me he leaves a wet print on the spot where his hand touched the table-top; not whiskey, water. Jude has a seat and sips his drink. He shakes his head with the burn of the first swallow and from the tips of his hair droplets of moisture hit my face.

"Did you just get out of the shower?"

"No," he says, and folds his eyebrows down the middle of his forehead.

"But," I say, and then bite my tongue. Drops of water are making a puddle beneath him wherever he touches. Jude is melting. "What's happening?" I ask.

He fills his glass again and wipes his forehead. "When the war was ending," he says, but I interrupt him.

"What's happening here, I mean."

It takes him a moment. "I think this is about what's happening here. Eventually. Sorry. Listen." The rain begins to fall outside.

"There was a boy from Galveston, Texas, in my battalion," he says. "The boy really was just a boy, eighteen, a real slight guy. He had two or three wiry billy goat hairs growing from his chin, but not enough to start shaving yet. This kid was quiet and didn't fit in with the other soldiers so well, like me, so we were often lumped together at meals or on night patrols. He had a girlfriend back in Texas who he missed so badly that sometimes he'd howl like he was a wolf. And whenever I asked him, 'Why the hell are you howling?' he said it helped him get all the longing inside him on the outside. So I let him howl. I didn't tease him about it, though some of the other soldiers would. I thought the wolf-boy was fine because lots of people had strange reactions to the war and what they saw. A lot of us started to wonder why we were there at all. So being a wolf didn't seem so bad, not nearly as bad as what some of the other soldiers did."

Jude fingers the hairs on his arm. Where he touches melts some more. A pool of water forms on the table.

"But the wolf-boy," Jude says, "after some time in the desert, he started to forget the boy side of his personality. He started to become all wolf, and it was a little bit disturbing to the other soldiers. It was really disturbing to me because we were friends. Sort of. I still went on patrol with him, but the boy had stopped talking all together. In fact, the boy had stopped walking on two legs when he didn't have to. He'd carry himself on all fours, with his head bent low to the ground as if he were trying to catch a scent of something. Even then I still tried to give him the benefit of the doubt, 'Well, he just misses his girl. He'll be all right,' I thought. And I continued to think that until the day a group of us, wolf-boy, me, and twelve other soldiers, were sent on a mission into a town that had been all but destroyed by our missiles. The Iraqis had mined it up pretty good, too, so it wasn't a very safe place to be.

"The town was small and all we found there was twenty-three dead people and a radio that was picking up music from a station all the way in Kuwait. The radio music was creepy since the rest of the town was so quiet. I picked my way through the town alone because I didn't really trust the other soldiers to not trigger a mine. Our job there was to dig a grave large enough to fit the twenty-three bodies we had found and to cover the bodies up, because the bodies weren't the bodies of soldiers but civilians, and they'd been sitting there for a while, a couple of days.

"After searching the town we began to dig, and the digging took far longer than we had thought it would because the heat was too much in all the gear we had to wear. We decided to wait for the sun to set. Then we didn't have enough shovels, which happened all the fucking time, not having enough tools for the job, and so we had to dig in shifts.

"After about an hour on duty I gave my shovel to another soldier and walked away to get some peace. But all the while that damn radio was still playing. I walked outside the light of the soldiers' lanterns to try to see the stars 'cause in the desert the stars were the only thing that reminded me I was still here on earth. But I couldn't see shit that night because the town was still smoldering and the smoke was thick between me and the sky, like it was gelatin.

"I walked through the paths in town that passed between homes which no longer had roofs or walls. I was touching the warm walls that were mostly ruined. I was thinking about the land mines. I thought about the triggers on the mines, and I was so lonely that the mines' triggers made me think of a woman's clit," Jude said, and looked up sheepishly, his brow soaking wet with melt. "In the dark I thought of all the hidden clitorises and pressed myself up against the wall that was still warm from the day and the fires. I thought of the land mines like girls. I shut my eyes and imagined I heard myself fucking the mine. I heard skin against metal skin, a slapping, a slobbering, a huffing. I was fucking a land mine in my head and it felt good. It was so real that I could hear it. But then I opened my eyes and the sound was still there. I listened. The sound was real. It wasn't the radio. Someone was there, slobbering and huffing. I crouched. I thought there might be an Iraqi or a wounded soldier. On my knees I crept along the wall until I saw a light and heard the noise grow louder. I looked through the door from where the light was coming. It was the wolf-boy. He was huddled over an Iraqi girl who had been dead for two days. Her head had been raised up on a rock like a pillow and in her hand she was still grabbing a slip of paper. I guess it was something she'd been holding when she died and she was still holding it. The wolf-boy was licking her face and neck with his tongue. He was slobbering, huffing on her as if to lick the girl clean and whole again.

'What the fuck are you doing?' I asked him, and tried to run toward him, but there were broken bricks and all manner of shit between us. I grabbed at him though I didn't know what I was going to do if I caught him, but it didn't matter anyway because the wolf-boy kind of reared up and his mouth was just sick with blood. He howled and he pointed his fucking pistol at me, not too much like a wolf. He turned and he ran away on all fours, only, one of the four was holding a fucking gun." Jude demonstrates this with his fingers on the table. "The wolf boy ran straight out to a dry field of crops growing beside the town. The field really was dry, it was burnt so there was nothing growing in it except for these land mines buried there and the wolf-boy touched one of the mines and then I did see stars even though the night was too smoky for stars."

Jude wrings his face and hair. Drops of water fall on the kitchen linoleum.

He's never told me anything like this before. He's never told me anything about Iraq really.

Jude continues, "I spent the night walking through the town. The roads were clear and there was a grid pattern to the streets, but the blocks surrounded by the grid were nothing but piles of rubbish, no more buildings. When the sun started to rise I came across some of the guys from my battalion. They were huddled by a pile of rocks," he says. "The rocks looked like they had been particularly assembled, like a grave site or some sort of memorial. So I asked the soldiers, 'What have you got there?' There were five of them and each one was younger than me, closer to your age, I'd say, nineteen or so. 'It's a well,' they said, and stared at me until one of them laughed. 'Let's have a drink then,' I said. I was so tired and wrecked. The soldiers were smirking like smart-asses so I didn't want to tell them about the wolf-boy. One soldier passed me the rope and said, 'Go ahead.' He turned to look back at the other soldiers, and each of them began to laugh. I threw the rope down, dipped the bucket, and started pulling it back up." Jude again demonstrates how he pulled the bucket up, turning away from the table to do so, and I stare as moisture drips from his forearms. "I could taste how cold the water would be coming up from so far down. I was ready for a nice long drink but when I got the bucket up into the sunlight, I could see the well wasn't filled with water at all." Jude stops the pulling motion and turns to me. "It was filled with watery blood that smelled of rot. I dropped the bucket and could hear it clang against the stones inside the well. The soldiers were laughing, but I think it was just 'cause they were scared by what was in the well. The one I had been talking to said, 'At first we thought something religious was happening.' Some of the soldiers were religious, even fundamentalist," Jude says. "And so they always thought religious things were happening because they were nervous. They were breaking the Ten Commandments so close to where they thought the Garden of Eden was supposed to have been. There was an Army chaplain who told them, 'No, no. It's not Thou Shalt Not Kill. It's Thou Shalt Not Murder. You boys are OK.' But they didn't believe him."

Jude shrugs and takes a sip. "So the soldier told me, 'But it's not religious. Here,' he said. 'Look,' and he shone his flashlight down into the well. There were bodies. Maybe a family of them." Jude stops and looks at me. "Then the soldier, he said, 'We figure they must have jumped down in there when the bombing started. That or else someone dumped them there,' he said. I looked down into the well until I recognized what I was looking at, and from the tangle I picked out the pale under-part of one body's arm. Then, I remember, one of the soldiers said, 'Idiots,' and he started kicking at the side of the well.

"I turned without saying anything because I thought I might get sick. I walked away from the soldiers and what had happened to the wolf-boy and the people in the well, and after a while I knew I was walking away from the war because I had a feeling like I was filled, like if I saw any more my mind might spill out over the top and start evaporating in the desert. So I just kept walking."

"Where were you?" I ask Jude. He looks out the window at the rain.

"Somewhere southeast of the capital," he says. "I walked until the town spread out and disappeared. Then I kept walking. I walked so far that soon I could tell by the patterns the wind had left on the sand that no one had walked where I was walking for a very long time, and I kept walking, feeling a nice freedom, like maybe I could walk the whole world." Jude stops to refill his drink. "You need another?" he asks, but I haven't even begun to sip the one he already poured for me. I shake my head no and he continues.

"The small peaks formed by the wind was all I could see. Like tiny waves, each one. It was kind of like being able to stand in the middle of the ocean. The peaks were no larger than my hand and each one composed of thousands, maybe millions of grains so tiny that they approached invisibility. For a second I thought, I am not like all those grains of sand," and he points a finger down to the floor. "I am just a walker."

Jude nods and kicks his legs under his kitchen chair.

"I started to dig a small hole, and as I dug I changed my plan. I thought, Wait. Fuck walking. I'll dig my way home. Like the hole to China. I'll walk through the very center of the earth and that way, I thought, people will know that I'm different." Jude bends his head to whisper to me even though we are alone. I can smell his breath. He whispers because he feels guilty to say it. "I thought of how messed up every vet from Vietnam I know is and I was terrified to be like them. I didn't want to spend the rest of my life having to think always about the war, 'cause it scares me when I see old vets walking around wearing fatigues sometimes still, like forty-fucking-years after-the-fact." He stops whispering. He pulls his head back from mine. "I didn't want that so I thought I'd dig my way home and I'd be different, noble and removed. The war won't leave a scratch on me, I thought. It was stupid, this plan, the hole to China plan. It lasted about four or five minutes until my hands couldn't take the digging any-more, and I realized that China is not on the other side of the globe from the Middle East. The Pacific Ocean is. I couldn't dig through that."

Jude folds over his legs and traps his arms in his lap. Without using his hands he puts his lips on the side of the fresh drink before him and takes a sip without ever touching his hands to the glass. He slurps. When he sits up he says, "After an hour or two, I had seen nothing but sand for a long while, when I noticed something up ahead. It was a small gatehouse or a toll booth, a tiny cabin built of wood and glass with a flat metal roof. It was weird because there was nothing else around.

"For a second I thought that superman might swoop down out of the sky and duck into the deserted gatehouse in order to change back into Clark Kent. I looked up. 'Superman,' I said. I was going home with Superman? But there was no Superman, just the sun. So I had another idea. I looked under my shirt thinking well maybe I was Superman and all I had to do was duck into this tollbooth, but all that was there underneath my clothes was a white cotton government-issue undershirt. I was fucked. I was fucked and roasting. I went inside the gatehouse. It was no mirage. I knocked on its wood." Jude taps shave-and-a-haircut on the table and then he swallows some whiskey. "Maybe a superhighway had once passed over the desert, but now the superhighway had disappeared in some apocalypse that I had slept through and all it had left behind was its small tollbooth." He wrings his face and hair.

"What the hell?" I ask about the water, but Jude doesn't seem to notice. He just keeps talking.

"I kept walking. I wanted to see what was on the other side of the gatehouse, what had been worth guarding."

"Weren't you getting burned and thirsty?" I ask him.

Jude nods his head yes. "I wasn't feeling things one hundred percent. Just walking, happy to be away from the war. I thought about how my brain was getting cooked inside my skull and how cooking it would make it more tender. I wanted that. Plus the desert was all these gentle rolling hills that hid what lay ahead. They made me curious, so I could forget being thirsty and think about what was on the other side of the hill. And hill after hill just revealed more hills, until I reached the top of one."

Jude stops to sip and looks me in the eye. "Nothing I can say could explain what I saw, but my first thought was, 'UFO. It's a damn UFO.' I thought that was wonderful. I didn't have to dig home or walk home or wait for Superman because a UFO was going to fly me home." He stops and spreads his arms like a bird and makes a whistling noise to simulate flying through the air. "I stopped walking and stared down from the lip of the valley to where a solid wall of baked mud bricks rose straight up and out of the flat land. It towered. It was smack in the center of a tremendous fucking valley. It was larger than my eyes could see in one glance. It required multiple looks. This thing was as large as an entire city and the perpendicular it cut to the earth was such a sharp opposite angle from the desert that I felt nearly queasy looking up at it. Even when it dawned on me that it probably wasn't a UFO but more likely something really, really old, like a ruin or a pyramid, I still couldn't shake the idea that it was from outer space.

"So I walked down into the valley. I wanted to touch it because I thought that it might also be a mirage. It took

me the better part of an hour to reach the valley floor
and the distance surprised me, as my perception had been
skewed by how empty the desert had been up until that
point. When I finally got to the wall of this thing I put
my hand up against one of the bricks that made the wall
and that brick immediately sucked all the moisture left
in my body out, carrying it, I imagined, far back to the
center of this thing like a hive of bees would do for their
queen, like it hadn't been touched in years."

Jude holds his hand up to demonstrate. But to me it
looks like he is waving to someone standing behind me. I
turn quickly. I am still nervous. No one is there. He continues, "I brought my other hand to the wall and the heat
of the ruin that must have been sitting there in the sun for
centuries burned me so badly that I felt the burn in the
back of my calves. But I kept my hands there. I wanted
the wall to suck not just my sweat but all of me through,
too. Slurp my entire body back through the baked mud
bricks and into the center of the temple where it must be
dark, cool, and moist. I stood waiting for a burst of light,
or a flash of electricity, or something magical to happen,
something so that I would know I wasn't like everyone
else, just going along with the shit the government told
us. I waited but after some time I realized nothing was
going to happen.

"So I turned, pressed my shoulder to the bricks,
and walked along the wall instead. While I walked, the

distances in that desert seemed to grow, rather than shrink, like a cartoon where the illustrator had drawn two stretches of land, and once I had crossed one panel, he'd bring that panel in front of me again. The same waves of sand repeating over and over.

"Walking with my shoulder pressed against something as large and as old as the ruin, the war seemed tiny and the purpose of the war looked like a pinprick, like a damn dim light because people die so quickly already without war. I thought about how, to the ruin, people must be mayflies, measly, annoying mayflies and mayflies only live for one day. Then I imagined a war among the mayflies but anybody at all could see how stupid a war among mayflies would be. People die so quickly already.

"What I didn't know but figured out after I got home was that what I had found was a ziggurat. There's a number of these throughout Iraq. They're these ramped, tremendous spiral structures, like the pyramids. They were once temples. The one I had found was one of the best-preserved examples that there is because it had been rebuilt a few times throughout history. First in 2100 BC a king named Ur-Nammu built a whole series of ziggurats. Most are gone now, but that one had been lucky for a long time. That one was once in the city of Ur, a city that had been famous for its library. Ur," Jude says. "Urrrrrr. I like that name. That ziggurat was originally called *Etemennigur*, which means 'House whose foundation creates terror.' And that was true. And it seems incredible that the name could still hold true after 4000 years, but it did.

"Finally I finished walking one side of the ruin and turned the corner, starting down the next side. At first I thought that someone, a sergeant, was screaming in my ear. The wind was so loud on that side that I had trouble believing it was the wind. It yelled and hummed, deep and low as if it had come from inside a belly. Not like anything I've ever heard here," Jude says. "Then I saw why it was that loud. There was a hole, a gigantic hole in the ruin, and the wind was getting caught and disrupted as it tore across the hole, making this hissing or screaming noise, like a rip. The hole was a seam, kind of a canyon, or a sharp, jagged tear. The hole was unimaginable. It was a gulf that opened up the entire inside of the ruin. When I got there, I climbed down inside the hole and inside it was shaded and cool. I followed the seam of the hole as far as I could. Chunks had been torn from the ruin's walls. The bricks had exploded and had been tossed about like boulders. They were that large. I was scared that the bricks above me might crash down on my head so I walked in real slowly. Through one blast in the ruin that resembled the state of California, I saw another blast that looked like England, like one was inside the other. And I had a thought and it was, 'Cannibals.'"

Jude runs his finger over his top lip and smiles. "See, my thirst was deteriorating my thoughts. Plus I was fucked. I had a seat on a pile of debris. When I sat the pile moved so I jumped. It was just the mess settling, but it scared the shit out of me. I thought the whole thing was going to fall. There were loads of rocks and old mortar and sand in the pile. I was digging through it, thinking I might find some odd treasure but instead I found a cracked bomb casing that was almost as long as my forearm. It was stenciled with white paint saying, TED STAT and then below that in pencil was a handwritten message. FUCK YOU TOWLE HEADS! It said. They spelled it wrong. I couldn't believe that our country had blown a hole in a ruin that was probably one of the oldest things on earth."

Jude looks at me. "No one in Iraq even wears towels on their damn heads," he says. "I kept walking and that night I slept out in the middle of the desert with the UFO on one side of me and miles of nothing on the other. I took off my boots. I thought that was the proper way to get ready to die. I was hoping death would come find me that night.

"But it didn't. I woke in the morning and there were two MPs standing over me asking, 'Are you crazy? Are you a goddamn loony?' I didn't answer, so one of them kicked me. I said nothing, so they determined I had mental problems. They said anyone who would walk as far as I had must have mental problems. And so they took me to a field hospital where the doctors were under orders to get as many soldiers back out fighting. So first they said, 'Nah, this one's all right,' and I was like, 'Shit yeah, I'm all right.' But just when I was about to be sent back out to fight, the shifts changed, and a second doctor came on. She had to review my chart before I left and she saw things differently. She said I was suffering from post-traumatic stress disorder and that I needed to be watched around the clock. She thought I was getting ready to kill myself and I told her, 'Shit yeah, I'm getting ready to kill myself.' So she made arrangements for me to receive a medical discharge. She said she couldn't get me on a flight out just then 'cause the planes were for soldiers who might not make it, but she said that there was a hospital ship going back to the States, a ship where she thought someone would watch me around the clock. She said I could go home on that."

Jude puts his forehead down on the table as if the telling is exhausting him. He hasn't ever spoken so much.

"I'm sorry." I pet the back of his head so that he'll know it's all right.

"Don't do that," he says. I stop touching him. "No," he says. "I mean don't forgive me. I wouldn't forgive me if I were you." Everything is quiet except for the rain. "Do you understand why I couldn't go on?" he asks me.

"But you did. You went on, Jude. See. You are here. You went on, Jude. You were just doing your job."

"Umh," he says and exhales as though it hurts him. "There's more," he says. "I didn't go on," he says.

"Right." With sarcasm. "You're dead."

"That's right," he answers in all seriousness. "And you're a mermaid."

I never told Jude I was a mermaid before.

I stand to walk to the window. Jude stands also. He sounds like the rain when he stands because drops of water spill off him. "Why are you melting, Jude?"

"We have to hurry," he says, so I think he is going to tell me the rest of the story. "We have to hurry," he says again, as though he is nervous. I turn to hear the rest of the story but he does something very different than tell me the rest of the story. He pulls me toward him and wraps his arms around my back. He is soaking wet everywhere. He is melting and it rubs off on me. He puts his head in my neck and then quickly he picks me up and pushes my back up against the wall. I stand very stiff because I cannot believe what is happening. I think he is either going to kill me or start kissing me. He splits my legs open and wraps them around his hips.

"You're melting," I say, and then he does kiss me. He is drenched and his kisses leave a trail on me. After a moment I realize what is happening. I kiss him back, his arms, his chest, his neck. I lift his shirt and I can taste his scars. He puts his hand on the small of my back and underneath one of my legs. He pulls me even closer and I can't believe what is happening. He puts his thumb between my legs right up the front of me.

Everything is more than I could have imagined, like having a square ice cube in your mouth and you can't swallow it. You have to let it drip slowly down your throat. Having him this close after years of wanting him this close, smelling deep in his hair and it's not just *my* hair, my pillow pretending to be him, it *is* him. Tasting his ear and having it taste differently than I ever imagined. How exciting that waxy difference is after years of wondering what the inside of Jude's ear tastes like.

"Hurry. Then I'll tell you," he whispers very quietly in my ear, losing more of my clothes. There and there and there. I had never felt love in my lungs before. Jude looks like a horse. A seahorse. He is pushing up against me and inside me and every time I kiss him his lips are wetter than before. He is melting and he has been drinking so that I feel like I am rocking, like we're on the sea.

Even after, when we are sitting on his bed with our legs around one another. I pet his face and listen to his breath and cannot fall asleep because there is a foreign feeling in my veins, it is the feeling of finally getting what I wanted, and the feeling is colder than I ever thought it would be. The feeling won't let me sleep.

Eventually Jude lies back, and through the night he drips and drips. I stay awake listening for as long as I can. The drip, drip, drip of him is the last thing I hear before I drift off.

In the morning it is still raining. Jude is no longer in bed. When I fell asleep he was wrapped around me but now he is gone. I touch where he slept. "Jude," I call but get no answer. The rain is coming down hard and loud, not in drops but more like it is pouring. I wrap the sheet around myself to look for him. He is not in the shower. He is not in the kitchen, though I see the bottle of whiskey we started last night. Someone has finished it. Jude must have drunk the rest sometime in the night, because it wasn't me. I enter the living room to investigate. "Fuck!" I land with a crack. My feet slip out from under me and I land with a splash on my back, knocking the air from my lungs, landing in a puddle of water in the middle of the living room floor. I rub the arm that I fell on. I look at the ceiling, thinking Jude's roof must have a leak. The ceiling is dingy white, but dry and coated with the webs that dust makes. No leak. I sit up in the water. It smells familiar. The puddle is large, far taller than me. I lower my face to the water and, there, I have a terrible thought. "Jude?" I ask. I can see my reflection. "Is that you?" I touch my tongue to the water that has pooled on the floor. I taste it. It is.

THE SEIZE

Jude melted. He really melted all the way to nothing but water. I unwrap the sheet that is covering me and I lie back on the living room floor so that I can be in the puddle.

The night before feels so near I reach my hand behind my back, believing that I can touch it. As I lie in the puddle I can still feel Jude from last night and it feels so real, not made-up this time. I experience the memory as an electric shock of thought in my brain. I wonder and worry about this electrical discharge in a pool of water.

"Jude. Jude. Jude." I turn on my side so the water goes in my ear. I put my lips just on the surface of the puddle, without touching the floor. "Don't go," I say. I kiss Jude everywhere. I swallow him. I drink the water from the floor. I have to lap it the way a cat or a dog would. It is dirty with dust and sand and filth, but I drink it anyway, and when I can't get anymore with my tongue, I sop Jude up in the bedsheet and wring the last drops of him into my mouth. "Jude," I say once I finish drinking all that is left of him.

"We're getting out of here," I say. "Let's go." I find Jude's keys on his kitchen table. Underneath the keys on the table there is a pen and a letter written from Jude to me. The letter is tucked into an envelope where Jude has written on the outside:

THE REST OF THE STORY

I stuff the envelope into my jacket pocket, being careful not to fold or crush it. "I'll drive," I say. It will be hundreds of miles before I have to decide where we are actually going. For now we are just going south.

I feel buoyant. I feel light and ready. I feel like we are getting out of here and mostly I feel Jude inside me and it feels like love.

I look again in the rearview mirror, and quite suddenly there is a beautiful blue as though the storm finally broke. It is truly a gorgeous color. This blue is chaotic and changing. I recognize it immediately. "Jude," I say, and I point into the rearview mirror. "It's the ocean. It's coming up behind us," I say. I watch as the blue rises up like a tidal wave so quickly that I am certain it will catch up with us soon. "It doesn't want us to leave," I say. I check the mirror. "At first, I thought it was a bunch of cop cars chasing us with their lights on but now I can see that it is the ocean." I accelerate. "I don't think we can outrun the ocean but I'll try for your sake."

I watch the blue in the mirror. It is so beautiful that it is hard to look away. "Jude," I say. "Fuck the dry land. I am a mermaid." I turn to look at him, but Jude is not sitting beside me. "Jude?" I ask and stare at the empty vinyl seat where he should be. I reach my hand over to touch the empty seat. But I look too long. I collide and burst through the guardrail and then I am sailing down into a deep ditch beside the road. For a moment I soar through the air in Jude's truck and I figure that might be it, time for one last thought. And so I sit, holding on to the wheel, waiting for that one last thought to arrive. I wait as the truck's nose dips and lands like an explosion, followed by a deep silence. The crash is over. After a moment I open my eyes. I look out the smashed windshield and see smoke or fog in the rain. The fog starts to turn blue and finally a thought does arrive. I am still alive. That's the thought. Just then the truck breaks the silence. It begins to sizzle as though it is angry at the accident.

"Jude?" I turn and ask, but before I can get any response the water rushes in like a couple of police officers with their blue lights flashing, with their guns drawn. The water rushes in like a couple of police officers would rush in to surround the smashed-up car of some drunk people who are evading the law. The water is like two officers, one on either side of the car both with guns drawn and pointed at me. The first officer opens my door and it creaks after the crash. He points his gun into my neck. His hand trembles so violently that the barrel of his gun shakes, tapping the bone at the bottom of my jaw. We stay together in silence. The engine is ticking, his hand shaking between my neck and chin, until he finally asks me, "Will you get out of the car, please?" He drops the gun back to his side where it continues to shake. I slide out of the car accident.

"Jude," I say.

"Miss," the policeman says so softly I can barely hear him in the rain, "You are under arrest for the murder of Jude Jones. Anything you say or do—," the man says and continues, but after the word *murder* paired with *Jude* I stopped hearing. The water rushes in and throws me into the back of a patrol car that returns me to town, that passes close by the ocean so that I can smell the shore's scent of decay. I can hear how the waves sound like breathing or snoring until we drive past and the ocean wakes up and watches the police car go by.

"We almost escaped," I tell the sea.

And the ocean spits what it thinks, like a storm, "Don't you ever try that again."

BACK ON DRY LAND

In the back of the patrol car the seat is built as a hole. It is very low and dark so that both the outside world and the front seat are obscured. I can only see the back of the policemen's heads. One, the young one with the soft voice and nervous hands, has cut his hair back so that it rises up and bristles at attention, in the same way one would expect the spines of a porcupine to do. The other man, who is older and rounder, has only a corona of hair, short fibers that circle his pate and leave the wrinkles of pink rolls at the top of his neck exposed. That haircut is like a monk's. The monk does the driving. "Sorry, I was so nervous," the young cop says to him. "I never pointed a gun at an actual person before is all. Especially not a girl. But sorry. Now I've done it and I'll be all right," he says.

"I know you will," the monk says. "You'll be fine," he tells the young officer and adds as an afterthought, "I've been on the force thirty-two years and this is only the fifth homicide I've ever even heard of around here," he says. "You did fine."

"A homicide?" I say to the policemen, but they do not answer me. I think they cannot hear me back here in this hole seat. That or else they can't hear me because they are on the dry land. "Are you guys looking for Jude?" I ask louder. Still they don't hear me.

"How'd you know?" the young cop asks the older one.

"Her mother called us. She was worried."

I ask again louder, "A homicide? Jude is dead? My mother?"

"Miss," the monk-haired policeman says without turning around. He's driving, "It would be better for you if you didn't speak to us. You're all over his house. You're all over the body in the living room and, goodness, you're fleeing the scene in his truck."

"The body?" I ask.

"That's the part we still can't figure out," the young man says, and I have to lean forward to hear him. He turns to look at me and stares, making me feel trapped and awkward. He watches me through the metal grating between the front and back seat as if I were an animal. I can barely make him out. "We're wondering how—in a bone-dry living room—did you manage to drown the poor guy?"

So I stop talking.

REST

Inside a small cement room with a wall of one-way glass they say, "Tell us what happened." The one-way glass seems extremely serious, and I find it hard to believe that such a formal room for interrogation would be wasted on me. I didn't kill anyone.

"Tell us what happened." It is the monk and the young one. They have a tape recorder.

There is quiet for a long time while I think. They want the whole story I guess. OK, the whole story. "Once upon a time," I begin. "Far, far below the deep blue sea—"

The monk stands to leave. "I see. You are going to play the crazy card. I'm not buying it. We'll come back when you are ready to talk."

They both stand and stare again. "I don't like it," the young guy says. "She's spooky. Her skin is so pale I feel like I can see through her," he says. It is the first real thing that has happened today. He can see me. What the young man says works like a door or window opening. It lets the policemen in, for real, and it makes me wonder, "How did you cops get inside my story?" I say it out loud, as a whisper, but out loud.

"What are you talking about?" the young man asks.

"Your story?" the monk asks. He smiles. "You are the one writing this story?" he asks, and slowly I nod my head because I can't tell if he is making fun of me. "If that's the case then you must know what happened to your friend Jude. You know, if *you're* writing this."

"He melted," I say but they stand to leave as if they don't believe me. "Wait. Wait," I tell them and then I say, "Jude wrote something, too."

"This?" the officer says and takes Jude's letter from a plastic evidence bag.

"Yes. The rest of the story. Yes."

"Your friend Jude is dead," the monk says. "Tell us what happened," he says and I look at his request. It looks like lead that he wants me to turn into gold.

"I didn't kill Jude," I say. "I couldn't have. Jude was already dead." And then I pull the letter Jude wrote me from its envelope. I hold it close to my heart.

I read them Jude's letter.

I'll write it here cause if you have it written you can look back over this 'til the letter falls apart and maybe by then you will believe me.

At first I felt lucky to be on the hospital ship. I was happy to be out of Iraq and going home. I wouldn't have been so happy had I known what the ship would be like. There were all manner of men missing arms and legs and eyeballs and noses and even one missing his center. His stomach had been blown out and somehow he had lived. They had replaced his stomach with a plastic bag where the doctors could watch to make sure the mush he ate was being digested. Despite the doctor's orders I wasn't watched all the time. I wasn't really watched at all. There were too many other soldiers who needed help. So I was more or less free to walk around the ship. And I did.

Belowdeck it was easy to become disoriented because the hallways were long and indistinct. It was especially easy to be disoriented since I already was disoriented. The walls in the ship's hallways were made of iron that met the floor and the ceiling in thick bumpy welds that looked like scars and each time I got lost the iron halls felt like corrals that said, "Behave, soldier, behave." I was sick. On that ship I thought I'd have a fit from claustrophobia. That and feeling that the reasons why we'd waged a war were loose and shifting daily nearly made me really lose my mind.

*I tried to think of home but I felt trapped and I felt
like the longer I stayed on board the deeper I sank in
complicity. Not that I wasn't already in deep. The only
relief I felt was when I could hear the ocean beating
the hull and know that the U.S. military did not own
the water. Yet. Everywhere there were sick soldiers.
There was vomit. There was blood and crying through
the night. We were wrecked. All of us. And the only
good thing I thought was that the waves could wash
it all away.*

*I remember striking my elbow on the pointy corner
of an iron stair railing and I didn't feel anything.
I puked and I didn't feel anything. So I cut my arm
with a shaver as a test and I still didn't feel anything.
And that feeling—the feeling of having no feeling—is
the most terrifying thing I have known. I thought,
"I'm dead. I'm already dead," and so barely, without
barely making a decision, I decided. I went up on deck
and I jumped overboard.*

*It was the coldest ocean I have ever felt, far, far
colder than here. The pain it gave me was good at first
because I could feel it and feeling something, even
freezing cold, battering waves was better than feeling
nothing. For one moment of pure fear I forgot the war.
The waves were tremendous. My ship was already
gone and I floated for a minute or two before realizing
what I had done. It crept up on me slowly. Feeling*

began to return. I thought of you. I thought how
I'd never see you and I couldn't believe how fucking
stupid I had been. I couldn't fucking believe it. I'd
survived the fucking war and now I was going to die.
From the trough, the very bottom of a fifteen-, maybe
an eighteen-foot wave, I changed my mind. I knew
even an ocean full of water couldn't clean away a war.
"Help," I yelled, just as a wave broke on me. Like who
the fuck was going to hear me? It took me under.

And here is what you won't like or won't believe
or at least you won't believe that it took me this long
to tell you, but your father was there. Your father was
the wave that took me under. "Help," I said again, but
I was in the tumble of the salty wave and your father
smirked. "I'll help you," he said. "You son of a bitch.
We'll make a deal. I'll save your life; you stay away
from my daughter. Forever." He said it. He didn't
want you to ever marry a mortal like he'd done. He
wanted you to come back to the ocean with him. He
said you are a mermaid.

I made a mistake. I agreed because I wanted to
come home from the war so badly. I agreed. But then
your father said, "I'm going to give you something
to make sure you stay away from her." And he took
a curved fishing knife and he cut my chest open. He
made me take it. He cracked my ribs apart so I knew
I was not only drowned I was dead. And your father

left something inside me that was even colder than the water. It was ice.

It happened. I know you won't believe me, but sometimes people come back from the ocean. The polar explorer, he was in a wave over 198 feet tall and he came back because he had all those men to rescue. And for some reason I came back, even a coward like me.

I woke up the next morning in my berth and at first I thought that was the clearest, oddest fever dream I'd ever had until I fingered something on my chest that hadn't been there before. White scars raised in a scribble across my entire torso.

He gave me an inside of ice so I'd never love you. But it didn't work. You are so close. You are sleeping in the next room. You are the only warm thing to me. So warm, I am melting.

Jude

UNDINES

In prison there are guards who speak only as chisels. They say, "No," or, "No!" or, "It's too late for that," or they say nothing. They won't answer. I quickly see what this type of chiseling can do to a life. One prisoner, a woman from even farther north than me, once was

a daughter named Edwina

a son Desmond

a false panel in the floorboards for hiding money a seamstress

at night, a recurring dream of eating grass

a visit, years ago, to Mexico

certainty

a leather sofa where she felt safe

a new mortgage

something her dead brother once told her

But the guards go to work on any life deposited in this sedimentary manner. They chisel into your recollection and, even worse, your dreams at night. They chisel into your children. Their purpose is to strip away all other frequencies of reality. They chisel and separate the layers of prisoners' lives so that all that is left is, "You work for me now. You do as I say." That is the only reality for many of the women here, to please the guards, to please the law. But I arrived in convolutions, more igneous than sedimentary, that is, mixed up. There was no way for them to strip away my reality without killing me. It was twisted inside me like a fetus.

Prison is impossible for me to imagine even sitting inside it. It is the poorest place on earth because control attempts to live here like a king. Control paves the yard outside. Control doles out violence and prescription drugs. Control poisons the tiny mice that sometimes run down the alleys between cells. The mice are the only beautiful things that still can live in prison. But control is fixing that problem.

I've seen the ocean once since I've been here. It was on TV, in the background of a program filmed in Southern California starring a team of lifeguards. It curled. It advanced and retreated. It tried to kill three children but the lifeguards got in the way. I have never been so sad.

The word *prison* shares a root with the word *surprise*, from the French *prendre*, *pris*—to take. I am not at all surprised by this. I think prison has taken Jude because I don't feel him inside of me anymore. I think prison has taken him. That or else I lost him because I cry all the time here and it tastes like him. I have a Dixie Cup that I harvest my crying into so that later I can drink it, in case Jude is in there.

Another prisoner here, a woman named Darlene, who is two years older than me and is being held in a cell next to mine for killing her husband, has asked me, "So what's your defense?"

"I don't have one," I tell her. "I didn't kill him."

"But you need one," she says. "Everybody here's got one."

"I don't," I say and think, "Oh, great. Prison has taken my defense, too." They take everything.

My mother comes to visit me. We are allowed to sit at a table together, not touching. There is no glass partition the way there is in the movies or in men's prisons, but still we are not allowed to touch each other.

"Why did you call the police?" I ask her first, and she starts crying.

"I was scared. I was so, so scared. You won't ever know what being scared is like. Only mothers can really know." She looks away as though she might even be angry at me if I don't understand. "You ran out and then you didn't come home." She is still looking away and I am afraid she'll leave me here. I ask her how long I have been here and she says, "Just three days now." I can't believe that. It feels like months.

"I saw the ocean on TV," I tell her.

"That's the saddest thing I've ever heard," she says.

"I know. I have to get out of here," I say.

"Well, what's your defense?" she asks.

I look up at her sharply. "I get that question a lot here."

"Well?" she says.

I look away. "Um, I didn't kill Jude," I say. "That's all I've got," I say.

"Hmm." She pulls her hair behind both her ears as if to hear better, as if hearing better will provide us with a greater choice of defense. "Hmm," she says again, apparently because when she listened she didn't hear anything.

"I have an idea," I say, and so she raises her eyebrows to listen. "You have to tell Dad that I'm here."

Her fingers clench, scratching the surface of the table. "Your father's dead," she says.

"On dry land he is dead. On dry land."

"Well, on dry land is where you live," she says.

"I didn't kill Jude," I say again and then start to explain. "In the war, Jude," I say and tell her the whole story. I even tell her about his letter and the torso made of ice.

"He said that about the ice?" she asks when I'm done, and I nod yes. "That's strange," she says, and reaches her hand forward, in between us as though she can remember what it feels like to touch a torso made of ice. "There is a certain similarity between the two of them," she says and then lowering her hand and looking away she says, "Maybe it is for the best that they are gone."

I don't say anything.

She shakes her head as though she is waking up. "Ugh. That's the dreariest story I've ever heard," she says. "That's one thing I've never liked about Jude," she says. "Dreary. I'm going to call a lawyer from the dry land," she says. She watches me while she stands. She hugs the air in front of her and, closing her eyes, she pretends she is squeezing me in her arms. When she leaves I am returned to my cell, and there the door is locked in place by a secret mechanism that I can't see.

The cell block where I am kept is extremely loud. The noise seems to be a quality that is built into the architecture. I rest my ear against the cinder block wall and I can hear all frequencies of conversation, sleep talking, chatting, even the sound of humming.

"Hello down there," one voice says, though I can't tell which direction it is coming from. The cinder blocks diffuse the location of the sound's origin.

"Hello?" I say softly, barely moving my mouth. At first I am embarrassed by the thought of placing my lips near the cinder blocks and speaking. I am wary that the guards will pass by and take something from me as punishment for talking. I am wary that the guards will take my voice, that a guard will turn the key to my cell and then use the same key to open my throat and remove a small box from there, that only later I will discover was my voice.

"Oh, the new girl!" another voice says in the wall, surrounded by the sounds of many sighs and exhales and giggles. I pull my head quickly back from the wall. It's alive, I think, and press my hand to it, expecting the surface of the cell wall to be fleshy or porous or at least electrically charged. It is none of these. It's concrete. I reapply my ear. The wall still sighs and giggles and whispers. "Is she there?"

"What's she in for?"

"Same as the rest of us," one voice says. And then another particularly loud voice cries, "MAN! SLAUGHTER!" and the wall fills with laughing.

"Are you there?"

"Did she go?"

"New girl. New girl."

I tap the wall. I put my mouth close to it. "I didn't do it," I say.

"Oh, she's coy. I love that in a new girl."

"I really didn't," I say. "Really. Really. Really. Really. Really." I hit my head against the wall each time I say it. Really.

"All right. All right," one voice says, though I hear others in the background mumbling, "Sure you didn't," or, "Liar," or laughter.

"Hmpf," I say to the wall.

"Don't listen to them. They are just bitter. They didn't do it either."

I pull my head away. If I had a pen I'd write on my hand, "Didn't do it," so that I won't forget. Next time I see a pen I will do this.

I put my ear to the wall again. Someone is saying, "New girl, tell us your story."

"Yes please."

"We're tired of all the other stories here."

"Yes heard them all and I mean HEARD! THEM! ALL!"

"Tell us yours."

I rest my forehead on the wall. "Shh," one voice says. "She's thinking," as though she could see me or as though the walls were not just a conduit of voices but a conduit of thought as well. I begin to wonder about all the voices. Were they all coming from inside the prison? Were they in my head? Or is the wall a repository? Maybe it holds onto the echo of old voices. Maybe some of these voices had already been released from prison or died and the wall is still reverberating with the sound of them. In that way the wall gave me no fear but rather comfort, because the wall felt like my house, old and haunted. I push my ear against the wall. The women are waiting for me to talk.

"One night," I begin, and close my eyes, "my father, he was very handsome, he walked into the ocean. That was eleven years ago. He hasn't come back yet and even though the police found the place on the beach where my father's footprints disappeared into the water, they never found his body. So my mother and I have been waiting. We often sit and wait on the beach just at the spot where they say my father's footsteps disappeared into the water. Sometimes I wait alone. We always thought he would return, and when I was young I would imagine the treasure he would bring back for me, starfishes or shark's teeth or the navigational equipment from a sunken fishing boat. One day while I was waiting for my father alone, I saw a man. He was in the ocean. He was very handsome. However, he was not my father.

"I fell in love with this man even though I was only twelve years old and he was twenty-six. His name was Jude."

"Jude," says one voice.

"Jude," says another, carrying the name further away through the wall.

"Jude."

I continue with the story. "I fell and fell and fell until I was so deep in love that love resembled a well, steep sides with no way out. Everywhere I looked and everything I saw was Jude.

"Jude had been a soldier in the war and when he came home he was different. As if the war had drilled a small gulf in him that no one could touch, no one could fill. He tried though. He tried to fill the gulf with drinking. He drank a lot."

I listen and there is no sound from the wall. I imagine the prisoners' heads pressed up against the wall, listening to me, their eyes closed, their thoughts escaping for a few moments. I consider what parts of my story I will leave out. I will leave out a lot. I will leave out the personality test. I will leave out, "I save your life, you stay away from my daughter." I will leave out how the ocean had me arrested.

I clear my throat, "A week ago I woke up at Jude's. I couldn't find him. He wasn't in bed. I looked in the bathroom and the kitchen. I looked in the living room. That's where I found him, only he was really different." I pause a moment, unsure how to tell them this part. It seems there's only one way to say it. "Jude had become a puddle, a puddle of water. And so, I was very confused at the time, I drank him."

For a moment the silence continues until the other voices realize I am done and slowly they begin to speak again. "That's the most romantic story I've ever heard," one voice says and I smile because I agree.

"Lovely."

"Sad," says another. I agree.

"You should talk to Undine," one voice that sounds maternal says.

"Who?" I ask. "Why?"

For minutes there is no answer. I hear a tiny laugh far away and finally the maternal voice returns, coughing before she speaks. "Undine is a mermaid, too."

I breathe quickly. I blink my eyes. Too? "How do you know I'm a mermaid?" I ask the wall but this time I really get no answer.

The maternal voice continues, "She's not here anymore, though."

"Where'd she go?"

Giggling. "She escaped."

"She did?"

"Yes, she really did."

"How?"

"Hmm. I don't know. None of us know."

"I know," one high voice says.

"No you don't," another prisoner tells her and then adds, "dummy." The high voice believes this is hilarious.

The mother voice speaks over the high laughing. "She had a similar story though. She had a husband, but after a few years the husband fell in love with Undine's stepsister. So Undine, the way she told it, went back down under the water. Her husband never really knew how miserable she was. Her husband never knew she was a mermaid. Then, at least the way she told it, her uncle made her do it, made her come back from the ocean and get the husband. She got him. At least the way she told it, she just kissed him but that's not what the pathology report said. It said he drowned."

The wall is very quiet.

Until one mean, deep voice cracks, "Sounds like you, girlene. Freaking mermaids."

I back away, suddenly scared that someone who shouldn't have been listening was listening, like the guards or the policemen. I take my ear away from the wall and find my bed with my hands. I try to sleep but thoughts of the women in the wall keep me awake. "That was a dream. That was a dream," I think, even though I know it wasn't. My face can still feel the wall's rough surface imprinted on my cheek. I know it wasn't a dream because while I am trying to convince myself that it was a dream, I fall asleep.

THE WAIT

I don't do anything in prison, and in fact I save and savor the few motions and things that I have to do during the day, holding out as long as I can, waiting, for instance, to brush my teeth, knowing that once I've done it, I'll have even less to do that day.

My mother visits me every single day. Sometimes she brings my grandfather, but it disturbs him to the point of befuddlement, to the point where he says things that depress us even more. Things like, "We have to go, Marcella's cooking a roast tonight," or, "What are we doing here?" or, "I left the word _____ at home," and he won't say the word because he left it at home. After a few visits, she leaves him at home.

My mother believes I am innocent, and not because the facts line up into a good defense but just because she believes me. For this I am extremely grateful. While she is here, I feel natural again. But her visits are limited to one hour, and so I have one hour of feeling natural, and twenty-three hours in which the only thing I have to do is brush my teeth twice and feel unnatural.

At night I speak to the wall, or at least I listen to it, and in the day I keep to myself and wait.

The sun rose earlier today than usual, I think. Not that I would know. I can't see any windows from here.

Still waiting.

Today I thought about the word *today*.

Applying wait like a person might apply herself to a job.

Wait.

Wait.

Something is moving.

No. I was wrong.

The faucet in my cell has a drip, and today I counted 2,908 drips while I waited. That's about one drop every fifteen seconds for twelve hours.

That's a lot of water.

So much that it gives me an idea. I construct a temporary drain plug made of toilet paper, and the water begins to collect, very slowly, but that is good for my purpose. I spend the day by the side of the basin and with every new drop that falls I say, "Dad, I'm in prison. Come get me." By seven o'clock at night the sink is full with, "Dad, I'm in prison. Come get me." I pull the plug and send my message out to sea.

I get in bed early. I am exhausted from being so vigilant all day. My cheeks and jaw hurt from having spoken so much. I am exhausted because all the hope I felt while filling the sink seems to have disappeared with the water down the drain. So, though I'd like to hope that my message makes it to my father, there's no hope left. I get into bed with anger. "Even if it gets to him he'll probably be drunk." I fall asleep.

Asleep I have a dream and in the dream I hear a bird chirp and warble. It is lovely. I pull a pad and pencil from my pocket. That is how I know I am dreaming—I am allowed a pencil and paper. On the pad, with my ear sharply tuned to the bird call, I begin to sketch a hirundine syrinx, that is, the vocal cords of a swallow. That is how I know I am a scientist, because I have never even heard of the word

hirundine–adj. of or like a swallow

before. When I have completed this sketch, in the dream, the syrinx I drew begins to chirp and sing and coo. That is how I know I am a real scientist. I collect my dream thoughts a moment. Then I collect a few choice science tools from a cabinet in my cell I had not noticed before. I choose a few pieces of equipment that I will need for my next experiment. I choose my Doppler profiler, my conductivity-temperature-depth recorder, a compass, and the salinity sonar. It is a heavy load but it is a dream and I have no trouble bearing the weight.

I stand at the door to my cell and, exhaling, I push the steel bars out of my way. Without fear, I walk through the hallway, turning left and right until I am standing before the prison gate. The gates bang with openness.

In the dream I carry my science equipment down to the sea. I will use it to pinpoint the exact location of Jude. I will take Doppler readings. I will make salinity profiles. I will graph the results until I arrive at an exact reading, the longitude, the latitude, and the depth of Jude in fathoms and feet. I will conduct an experiment to measure whether the ocean is good or bad, because I have a hypothesis that it is neither. I think I can prove that as a scientist. I take my Doppler profiler in hand. I imagine presenting my results to the world, and how in light of the startling results, the government will fund a study to prove the same thing about humans—that they aren't necessarily good or bad—and if I could prove that I could pull Jude back up through the war and the water. I could make him mine.

In the dream I touch my toe to the ocean and the shock of the cold water is lovely. It feels like breathing. Unfortunately the shock of the cold water is really a shock and it wakes me up.

When I wake I am in prison. There is no cabinet of scientific equipment. It is dark and still and I am only momentarily confused. I remember the ocean and that it was a dream, but rather than feeling defeat what I feel is a residue of water that is so strong I imagine my toe feels wet and that thought makes me smile. I reach for my toe in the dark.

My toe is wet.

I bolt upright and the cot squeaks. "Shh!" I tell it. I get out of bed. At the end of the hallway of cells there is a red EXIT sign. It is required by law, though it has often been the source of amusement among prisoners, as there is not actually an EXIT open to us. The sign glows very brightly at night and casts a red glow down the hallway. I grab onto the bars of my cell and see that the red is reflecting off something in the alley between cells. The red light is caught in a trail of water that leads to the door of my cell. I can see where each of his feet fell because there is a print of water and the water reflects the red of the EXIT.

I pull my hair as a test. It hurts.

My ribcage grows tight, making it difficult to breathe. For one moment I look back at the bed, but only for a very quick moment. I try the bars. They glide soundlessly, and in my bare feet I follow my father's wet prints.

BLUE

I run and run and run through the hallways of the prison. At first I think, "If I run fast enough I will catch up to my father." But the faster I run, the harder it becomes to breathe. This stiffening in my lungs is a question that is pounding and growing and taking up space. The question is, "What do you mean catch up with your father? Catch up to being gone?" I stop running. People die so quickly already.

When I reach the gates of the prison the sun is coming up. The gates open to let me out and there on the other side of the prison gates is my mother, waiting beside our car with the engine idling. I run and quickly jump in. "Come on!" I holler. "Let's go!" My father must have told her to come get me.

She turns slowly back to the car and gets in. She reaches across the gear shift to hug me. "Baby," she says. "My poor baby."

"Come on, Mom. We better hurry before they realize I'm missing."

"Huh?"

"What happened? Did Dad come tell you?" I ask.

Her face wrinkles, like sadness and confusion were a blanket covering it all of the sudden. "It wasn't your father. Oh." She looks away from me but still does not put the car in gear. "The police called," she says. "They said you were free to go. They said there was a note, a suicide note. They said you weren't responsible. Oh." She holds onto the wheel until her flesh whitens. "They said Jude killed himself."

My mother and I both stare straight ahead, waiting.

The prison is surrounded by very tall pine trees. And after my mother says this, the trees and the prison continue to stand, sturdy and appropriately in the middle of a dark forest that keeps all the dark secrets of a forest. Birds, squirrels, fog, deer bones buried under pine needles, and lichen. Jude killed himself. The possibility that this might be the truth swoops near my head like a bat at dusk, a bat that soon flies off in the other direction uninterested in me.

Jude's note. I smile. He really fooled them.

"Mom." I say, "Listen," and begin to tell her about the drip. I tell her about the drain and the dream and the noiseless way my cell door slid open. "There were wet footprints and I followed them. It was Dad," I say and after thinking a bit, biting my lip, I add, "And that is the truth no matter what plain or boring or painful excuse you choose to believe instead."

"I don't know what to believe just now." She exhales. The word *just* gives me hope that she might believe me. *Just* seems more like a moth just passing through and once its gone she'll believe me that Jude and my father are alive. She'll believe that I am a mermaid and her life won't be so dreary. I keep talking. I tell her about the other prisoners and how we got fed and showered and exercised like horses. I tell her about the mice and the poison the guards set out for them. I tell her details. Details make a story even as unbelievable as mine believable. My mother stares straight ahead at the prison, nervously fidgeting with the skin of her thumbs. I continue telling her about the police and the guards until she doesn't want to hear anymore, until she is full.

"Ugh," she says shaking her head no. "That's not how it ends," she says. "I've read enough books to know that's not how it ends."

"Tell me how it ends then."

She squints her face up, thinking, trying to be very careful about the words she chooses. "It's harder to say in words," she says. "Words are so precise."

"Why don't you say it in sign language?"

"You don't speak sign language."

"I'll understand," I tell her.

And so she does. Her hand bobs up and down, like a fish swimming. Her fingers flare out slightly as she rises from each dip with words flying off them.

"Ah," I say when she is done and for all I know it could mean, "Look out! Disaster!" But I don't think so. I think it's closer to Ocean. Continue. Forever. Smooth night with stars for navigation.

Words have more than one meaning all the time. Just like Jude's note.

"Mom, listen to me for once without thinking no, no, no. OK?"

She nods and tears at her lip with her teeth.

"It was Dad," I say. "He helped me escape."

She doesn't speak. She puts the car in gear and pulls away from the prison. She stays silent for awhile while we pass out of the pine trees.

"Where is he?" she finally asks.

It takes me a moment to answer because I don't really know. And in that moment her bottom lip starts to shiver.

"I think he went back to the ocean."

She nods her head and looks down.

"Do you want to go see?" I ask. "Maybe—" But I am nervous to finish my sentence, to say, maybe he's there. Her lips tremble so much she begins to cry. She doesn't answer me but turns our car away from our house. She points us towards the sea.

"What about you then? Are you going there too?" She wipes her tears on her sleeve and shoulder.

I don't have an answer to that yet.

"Maybe it's time for both of us to go," she says. I don't think she means to New York.

The sun is just coming up and it is turning the sky a beautiful shade of blue. She keeps driving straight down to the ocean. We park and as I climb from the car all the small, dry, yellow flowers that grow like trash by the side of the sandy road touch my ankles. My mother and I walk through the flowers down to the ocean. When we see the sea I jump. I am so happy, because I think, "Jude, there you are." My mother cocks her head sideways, as though she wants to be happy but forgot how, and is only just now getting some vague recollection of what that felt like.

My mother and I reach the edge of the water and hesitate to shed our clothes for just a moment. We walk towards the water and we continue walking, right into the water. After a short while, we don't have to walk anymore. The water is quite cold but it feels like a deep breath.

"Woo! That's cold," she says and splashes the tears off her face with a handful of seawater. "Look out," she tells me, and smiles because a wave is building in front of us. The water is filled with words. This wave is

smelly–adj. having or giving off a foul odor

like the sea. We dive under it and the words rumble over our heads. When we surface my mother has caught **giving** in her hair.

"I didn't know you could break definitions," she screams to me but I don't answer. Another wave is coming.

> **wait–vt.** 1. to stay in one place or remain inactive 2.
>   to remain temporarily undone or neglected 3. to
>   serve food

We dive clear. We don't want any of that wave. "Of course you can," I say, and demonstrate as a small wave of **hysteria** passes.

> **hysteria–n.** Gr. hyster, the uterus 1. a psychiat-
>   ric condition, anxiety, fits of laughing, crying,
>   simulation of organic disorders such as deafness
>   or blindness

Floating over the wave I pick out **laughing** and throw it at her. "See," I say and this does make her laugh.

"How do you do it?" she asks me.

"I think it's like chemistry. Like the letters are atoms, the words are molecules, and the sentences are elements. You just choose what scale you want to see the world."

"I get it." She says. We begin to jump up and down as the next wave grows in front of us. It is large, growing larger as we watch. We swim directly through it.

> **lady–n.** from hlaf: loaf, and -dige from (bread)
> kneader 1. a woman loved by a man 2. a woman
> who has rights 3. a title

"Woo!" she shouts. In her hands she has grabbed **rights** and **loved** and **loaf**. She turns to show me the possibilities the definers never thought of. "Ha," she says, and her eyes widen to read something. "Look around your neck," she says.

I touch the word. It's a **title**.

"Is that what you want?" she asks.

I suppose so. I have been looking for a **title**. I hold onto the word.

We float on our backs, every choice, every word, every possibility is drifting somewhere nearby us. Somewhere nearby is Jude. Somewhere nearby is my father. Somewhere nearby are all the words the town will say about me. **Sad**. **Stupid**. **Suicide**. In time, my mother might get cold or tired. She might even go home, but for now we are happy right here. We let the waves roll beneath us and forget the dry land and forget the idea of ever going back because the water is

blue–n. Fr. bleu 1. having the color of the clear sky
or the deep sea 2. melancholy 3. puritanical 4.
obscene 5. faithful 6. said of women, especially
those with literary inclinations

If one word can mean so many things at the same time
then I don't see why I can't.

"Are you going to stay here?" she asks me again. But
I still don't have an answer. Instead I tell her, "In the
Arctic there's a string anchored to the bottom of the sea
at 13,681 feet. Along the string scientists have attached
their instruments: sonar to measure ice caps' thicknesses,
vanes to measure current, a conductivity-temperature-
depth recorder, and a fluxgate compass since regular com-
passes don't work so near to the magnetic pole." And then
I ask her, "How do I know this if I'm not a mermaid, if I
don't belong in the ocean?"

"Maybe you're a scientist."

"Maybe I'm both."

"Maybe," she says. "Maybe you're just good at making
things up."

"Maybe."

The polar explorer's shipwrecked men waited and waited
for weeks, existing on ice and little else. They had sent
their beloved leader off on a rescue mission, but the horizon remained unbroken and some men had secretly given

him up for lost. By noon some men felt a surrender set in, a surrender that oddly felt a bit like joy. One man removed his boots so he could feel the packed snow between his toes. One man built a castle of ice and spent the day imagining it was real. One man secretly dragged a knife blade across his arm to make certain he was still alive. He was. Which is how he saw the ship. The steady line between sea and sky had been unbroken for days, days that had begun to pile up and wilt. "I must be getting snow blind," the man thought and turned his back away from the horizon. But something had lodged in his vision, the blue afterimage of a ship, a rescue ship. He turned back to the sea that he had, just moments before, considered walking into. He turned back to the sea and saw the tiny ship getting larger.

That is how I feel, only there's no ship, just the sea to rescue me.

Thank you PJ Mark, Masie Cochran, Maggie Nelson, Joe Hagan, Diane Hunt, Pat Walsh, and David Poindexter. The Story of Dangerose comes from Joseph T. Shipley's *Dictionary of Word Origins*.